Chasing Brooklyn

Also by LISA SCHROEDER

I Heart You, You Haunt Me
Far from You

Chasing Brooklyn

LISA SCHROEDER

Simon Pulse
New York London Toronto Sydney

This book is a work of fiction. Any references to historical events, real people, or real locales are used fictitiously. Other names, characters, places, and incidents are the product of the author's imagination, and any resemblance to actual events or locales or persons, living or dead, is entirely coincidental.

SIMON PULSE
An imprint of Simon & Schuster Children's Publishing Division
1230 Avenue of the Americas, New York, NY 10020
First Simon Pulse hardcover edition February 2010
Copyright © 2010 by Lisa Schroeder
All rights reserved, including the right of reproduction
in whole or in part in any form.
SIMON PULSE and colophon are registered trademarks
of Simon & Schuster, Inc.
For information about special discounts for bulk purchases,
please contact Simon & Schuster Special Sales at 1-866-506-1949
or business@simonandschuster.com.
The Simon & Schuster Speakers Bureau can bring authors to your
live event. For more information or to book an event contact the
Simon & Schuster Speakers Bureau at 1-866-248-3049 or visit
our website at www.simonspeakers.com.
Designed by Mike Rosamilia
The text of this book was set in Adobe Garamond.
Manufactured in the United States of America
2 4 6 8 10 9 7 5 3 1
Library of Congress Cataloging-in-Publication Data
Schroeder, Lisa.
Chasing Brooklyn / Lisa Schroeder.—1st Simon Pulse ed.
p. cm.
Summary: As teenagers Brooklyn and Nico work to help
each other recover from the deaths of Brooklyn's boyfriend—
Nico's brother Lucca—and their friend, Gabe, the two begin
to rediscover their passion for life, and a newly
blossoming passion for each other.
ISBN 978-1-4169-9168-7
[1. Novels in verse. 2. Grief—Fiction. 3. Nightmares—Fiction.
4. Interpersonal relations—Fiction.] I. Title.
PZ7.5.S37Ch 2010
[Fic]—dc22
2009019442
ISBN 978-1-4169-9882-2 (eBook)

For Michael del Rosario—
I couldn't have done it without you

Acknowledgments

It takes many, many people to make a book and then to get said book into the hands of readers. I'd like to take this opportunity to shine the light on the team of people who have worked tirelessly behind the scenes on my behalf. Please know I appreciate your work more than I can say.

A HUGE thank-you to:

The electric editorial team—Bethany Buck, Jennifer Klonsky, Mara Anastas, Anica Rissi, Annette Pollert, Emilia Rhodes, and Michael del Rosario.

The pristine production team—Carey O'Brien, Brenna Franzitta, and Ted Allen.

The delightful design team—Cara Petrus and Mike Rosamilia.

The marvelous marketing team—Lucille Rettino, Bess Braswell, and Venessa Williams.

The legendary library and education marketing team— Michelle Fadlalla and Laura Antonacci.

The perky publicity team—Paul Crichton and Andrea Kempfer.

The SUPERspectacular sales team, who are too many to list here unfortunately, and a special shout-out to Victor Iannone for his enthusiasm and Jim Conlin because the third book might not be here if it weren't for his incredible support of the first.

One year ago today

I lost my boyfriend, Lucca.

He was
an artist
like me,
a dreamer
like me,
a nature lover
like me.

We met in September
of our sophomore year.

By November,
he was my first
"I love you"
boyfriend.

Some thought it was impossible
after only two months.

I'd reply, love doesn't tell time.

Love is simply there
or it isn't.

Every day,
in every way,
it was there.

One year ago today

I lost my brother, Lucca.

He was a son,

a brother,

a friend.

The whole school was in shock when he died.

Just six months earlier,

another guy from our school died.

Everyone went on about too much tragedy.

Want to know about tragedy?

Come to my house.

A year later, tragedy is still here.

Every damn day, it's here.

It's early when I take flowers
to his grave.
I don't want to see
anyone else.

The yellow Gerber daisies
aren't flashy,
but beautiful in their own special way.
Like he was.

How many times
have I wondered
if he'd still be alive
if I had stayed home?

How many times
have I wondered
if there's anything
I could have done?

How many times
have I replayed
it all in my head?

More than there are
blades of grass in this cemetery,
that's how many.

Last New Year's Eve.
He said he'd be careful.
He said he wouldn't drink.
He said he loved me and he'd see me soon.

I was in North Dakota, at Grandma's, for the holidays.
We talked just a few hours
before it apparently happened.

In the early morning hours,
while I had sweet dreams
of me in his warm, loving arms,
my phone filled with messages.

Messages from friends telling me
my boyfriend was
dead.

#277

Dear Lucca,

I don't like cemeteries. Although, does anyone really like cemeteries? I mean, really? So many dead people, and they're just creepy. But here I sit in one, writing you a letter.

I remember one year when I was six years old, Daddy drove me through a cemetery Halloween night. He said when he was younger, he liked to have spooky fun in a graveyard. I was excited, until we got there and walked around. He told me we might get lucky and run into a real live ghost. I turned around and ran back to the car as fast as I could, crying so hard I thought I was going to throw up.

But for you, I'll do anything. Hope you like the daisies.

Love always,
Brooklyn

I go by myself

to see Lucca.

Ma will be too loud,

wailing for him to come back,

as if Heaven will hear her cries and do as she says.

Yellow daisies tell me Brooklyn's been here.

His flower girl.

I brought nothing.

Just myself.

Seems fitting.

Feels like that's all I've got anymore.

At home, in my room

I pull out the shoebox
filled with Lucca
keepsakes.

Notes passed
between classes
with words of adoration
and little cartoons
telling the story
of me and him.

Love

Pictures of us
smiling
making faces
kissing
around town
one sunny afternoon.

Joy

Ticket stubs
from time shared
together at
plays,
movies,
concerts.

Happiness

After a while,
I put the box away,
the love,
joy,
and happiness
right along with it.

On the way home

I stop at the park

where we used to

run

slide

swing

jump

boys being boys,

our happiness measured

by how far we could jump from the swings.

Today I swing,

my legs pumping hard and fast

to that magical place where it feels like any second,

my feet will touch the clouds.

But this time, I don't jump.

I

        just

            stop

pumping.

I grab my Lucca notebook
and make the weekly trek
to Another Galaxy.

Lucca loved going to
the comic book store
where the shelves are filled
with the best of
art and storytelling.

It was his home
away from home.

Now, I find strength in the pages
of the skinny little books.

Who doesn't love to see
characters overcoming
the greatest of odds?

So I go, combing the boxes,
picking up a couple each week
with some of my allowance.

I keep them by my bed
and when I can't sleep,
I pull a comic out
and hope a little of the
courage and strength
comes to me
through the pages.

Tom Strong is my favorite.
Sure, the story is good.
But it's his name
I love the most.

When I get to the store,
the sign says CLOSED.

New Year's Day.
A holiday.
I forgot.

The anniversary of the day
your boyfriend died
will do that to a girl.

Time for a run.

How far today?

Five miles?

Six?

It's only noon.

I have the whole afternoon.

Might as well go eight or nine.

"Don't you want lunch?" Ma calls after me.

I wave at her and head out.

Lunch can wait.

Everything can wait.

Time to run.

The walls of death

are closing in around me.
My best friend, Kyra, calls to ask
if I've heard the news about Gabe.

Gabe Gibson, Lucca's friend.
The driver that night.
The one who survived.

When she tells me what's happened,
her words hit me hard,
like a hammer to my heart,
I fall to the floor.

"Brooklyn?
Brooklyn!
Are you okay?"

It's hot.
Stifling.
Need. Air.

"Brooklyn!
Should I come over?"

I make it outside,
where the sun is setting,
the sky a canvas splattered
with vibrant red and orange.

Clouds stretch across the sky
like cotton balls pulled apart by a child.
It looks so soft, I close my eyes,
trying to imagine the sky
wrapped around me,
comforting me.

But it's impossible
to feel comforted
in this uncomfortable
moment.

"Brooklyn, speak now or I'm calling 911!"

"Kyra—" I whisper,
and that's all I can manage.

Every part of me feels
numb.

"I know," she says.
"I know. You okay?"

"No . . . no!
How could he…
I don't . . .
Are you sure?
I mean really?
God, I feel sick.
Was it an accident or—?"

"Don't know.
A drug overdose.
That's all they're saying."

My mind races,
a million questions
chasing one another,
eluding any
logical answers.

He lived.
He made it.
A second chance,
given to one
and not the other.
And this?
This is what he did with it?

"I can't believe it, Kyra."

"I'm so sorry, B.
I knew this would upset you."

"I gotta go," I say.
"I'll see you tomorrow."

As the red and orange
fade into grayness,
I can't hold it in
anymore.

I sob and think,
Why, Gabe?
Why?

I'm so pissed,

I can't stop throwing things.

I threw the Guitar Hero guitar across the room and
broke it.

If Lucca was alive, he'd be pissed too.

Except if my brother was alive,

his friend wouldn't have gone off the deep end,

so they'd both still be here

and there wouldn't be anything to be pissed about.

I don't care how guilty you feel about driving your car
into a tree,

you don't go and do something stupid like that.

Asshole.

I don't get it.

Was he trying to punish himself?

No. He didn't punish himself.

He punished

his bandmates,

his family,

a whole school.

A school that's had more than its fair share of grief.

I pace the floor, my heart racing while I resist the urge

to throw more stuff around.

Finally, I put on my running shoes.

I'll run until I can't run anymore.

Gabe was one of those guys

who was full of life.
Always talking.
Always laughing.
Always wanting to be the center of attention.

Big guy
with a bigger smile
and the biggest heart.

After Lucca died,
it changed Gabe.
Of course it would.

He went from front and center
to just fading into the background.

We hung out for a while
after it happened.
Didn't talk much.
Mostly we sat in his room,
me writing letters,
him strumming on his guitar.

Still, we promised
we'd help each other through it.

But then, something changed.
I don't know what.
Was it him? Was it me?

He joined a different band.
Stopped coming around.
I just lost track.
We lost track.

I try to remember
the last time I saw Gabe
and I can't.

He didn't just fade
into the background.

He pretty much
disappeared.

#278

Dear Lucca,

Can you believe this? I can't.

I can't believe he's gone.

Remember that one time the three of us went to see Kings of Leon? Gabe sang every song. He knew every single song.

I seriously feel sick. Gonna go lie down.

Love always,
Brooklyn

Gabe and my brother

had been friends

since fourth grade.

They'd grown apart in high school

when Gabe chose music

and Lucca chose art.

Still, they had that connection,

the kind that stays strong

despite the differences.

No matter how long it'd been

since they'd seen each other,

they'd pick up right where they left off.

Gabe made Lucca laugh like no other.

Gabe with his wild hair that stuck every which way,

his pierced lip

and the black leather jacket

he wore everywhere.

He was a character.

A character who should still be here.

Damn it all to hell.

He should still be here.

The principal holds an assembly.

He tells everyone he understands
how hard this is for us,
but we're strong and we'll get through this.

He tells us calls and e-mails
are pouring in from across the nation.

He tells us this time, counseling is mandatory.
Every student at Mountain View High
will speak to a counselor.

Three boys.
Three deaths.
One school.

We've made the national news.
Is our school cursed?
Are we a reckless bunch of fools?
The media asks questions
no one can answer.

Kids can't stop crying.

It's a downpour of tears
through the halls
for Jackson,
for Lucca,
for Gabe,
for all of us
who have to go on without them.

The helplessness in the air
is heavy,
and we walk around
with our heads and shoulders down,
feeling the weight of it all.

Teachers are going easy on us.
Most classes, we just sit
and talk
and cry.

In a few days,
we'll go to Gabe's funeral,
hoping to put this behind us
and move on.

Daddy said he'd go with me.
Mom went to Lucca's funeral with me.
But now that she's moved to Vegas
with my twin brothers,
he's the only one here.

When I told him about Gabe,
he didn't know what to say.
He looked at me, started to speak, then stopped.
Words vanished like the three boys.

So he wrapped his arms around me
and held me tight.

I know what he was thinking.
Don't go there.
Don't feel so bad,
you go there and
don't know how to get back.

I do feel bad.
My boyfriend left me.
My mother left me.
My brothers left me.

Hold on tight, Daddy.
You're all I've got left.
Please.
Hold on tight.

My parents

are friends with Gabe's parents.

They liked Gabe.

Now, the two of them huddle together,

whispering things,

Pop holding Ma up one minute,

Ma holding Pop up the next.

Gabe told them one time how sorry he was.

They hugged him.

Said they forgave him.

Guess he didn't believe them.

After Lucca died, everything shut down.

I couldn't eat.
I couldn't sleep.
I couldn't talk.

Somehow they got me on the plane
and back home.

Friends from school called and stopped by.
Even kids I didn't know stopped by.
All of them, wanting to help somehow.

I hated it.
I didn't want to see anyone.
I didn't want to talk to anyone.
But Mom made me.
She said it'd be good for me.

Of all the people who visited,
Ava stands out in my mind.
She brought me cookies and a CD she made
called *Joy, Not Sorrow.*

"The songs move through the stages of grief," she said.
"Someday you'll get to the place of joy.
Maybe not tomorrow or next week or next month.
But someday you will."

We didn't know each other.
I knew who she was because everyone knows.
She's the girl whose boyfriend, Jackson, died.
Now I'm that "other girl whose boyfriend died."
How special.

I don't remember much of what she said.
"Call me if you want to talk."
I never did.
"Lean on your friends and family."
Don't have much to lean on, really.

I remember when she hugged me,
I didn't want to let her go.
She was my budding crocus
on a dreary winter day.

I played the first half of the CD over and over.
Evanescence spoke to my soul with *All That I'm Living For.*
Jason Mraz spoke to my heart with *Dreaming to Sleep.*
The Williams Brothers spoke to my pain with
Can't Cry Hard Enough.

I never called her.
I probably should have.
But I never did.

I hear the word

in the hall

over and over again.

Suicide.

Suicide.

Suicide.

Did he or didn't he?

Everyone's got a guess.

Still no one knows for sure,

except Gabe,

but he's not talking.

Why does it even matter?

He's gone.

His, ours, theirs—

blame needs a place.

His, ours, theirs—

pain all over the place.

His, ours, theirs—

forgiveness missing from this place.

I want to go home.

I left my notebook filled with
letters to Lucca at home.

The blue spiral notebook
that used to be his,
with cartoon drawings
all over it.

It was in my locker
before he died.
He threw it in there after a class
and forgot about it.

So I kept it.
And now, I never leave it at home.
Wherever I go, it goes.

We belong together.
Without it, I can't function.
It's like missing a brain,
a heart,
or lungs.

My head hurts.
My chest hurts.
I can hardly breathe.

It's the middle of first period
when I notice it's gone.
I'm the first one out the door
when the bell rings.
Then I run all the way home
to get it.

#279

Dear Lucca,

The funeral is tomorrow. 1 don't want to go. 1
mean, 1 REALLY don't want to go. Daddy said 1
have to. He's making me. Says 1 need to go and say
good-bye.

What if 1 don't want to say good-bye?

Love always,
Brooklyn

A big woman,

Gabe's aunt or something,

is singing this sad song,

and people are searching for tissues

in the most desperate way,

like it's blood falling instead of tears.

Whatever.

I just keep looking at that coffin and thinking

about this song Pop belts out

when his beloved Notre Dame football team

stomps on an opponent.

Another One Bites the Dust.

Yeah.

Still pissed.

In a funeral home

there's no cross to give you hope.
There's no bible to give you peace.
There's no minister to assure you all is well.

In a funeral home . . .

There are still flowers which I love.
There are still people who I know.
There is still death which I hate.

In a funeral home . . .

There is a family without a son.
There is a band without a guitarist.
There is a school without a classmate.

In a funeral home . . .

There is a coffin with a boy.

#280

Dear Lucca,

Heading to Another Galaxy in a minute, imagining I'm meeting you there. What will we buy today, I wonder?

The funeral yesterday was sad. Like it'd be anything else. Anyway, I'm glad it's over. Still, I can't stop thinking about Gabe. How come no one saw it coming? I'd heard he was partying hard, but I just thought . . . I don't know what I thought. That he was dealing the best he could. Like we all were.

I hate this. Will the darkness ever fade? Will I ever see light again?

Is it light where you are?

Love always,
Brooklyn

My turn to talk to the counselor.

"How are you feeling?" he asks.

    "Not good."

"What do you mean, not good?"

    "Not good.
    As in bad.
    Angry."

"At Gabe?"

    "Yeah, at Gabe.
    And at you, for thinking you can help.
    And at my brother, for dying, which made Gabe want to die.
    And at everyone, pretty much."

"Do you envy Gabe at all?"

"Envy him?

Because he's not here anymore?

Because he doesn't have to deal with all of this?

Because he doesn't have to watch my parents,

barely able to hold it together?

Because he doesn't have to be around all these

stupid crying people?

Yeah, I guess I do.

I mean, he's got it so easy."

"Nico, do you know what that sounds like?"

"Like I wish I was dead?"

"Do you?"

I shake my head hard.

I bite my lip.

I think of everyone who has lost.

Like me.

And then, for just a minute,

I'm one of those stupid crying people.

When your mom tells you one day

that she's up and moving to Vegas
and taking her eight-year-old twins,
but not you,
it pretty much feels like you shouldn't have been born.

I wanted to know why.
I asked a hundred times.
She said she didn't have an answer that'd satisfy me.
"I don't love him anymore, honey.
Things have changed.
I've changed."

And that was that.

So when she calls once a week to talk
and to tell me she loves me,
but my dad needs me most,
I don't say much.

I just say yes or no,
answering her questions,
hoping she'll get the point
and stop calling.

She never does, of course.
She's my mom.
She's supposed to call.

Today, she asks me about Gabe.
Daddy must have told her.

"Are you doing okay?"

"Yes."

"Was the funeral sad?"

"Yes."

"Is it hard going to school?"

"Yes."

"Do you want to come for a visit?"

"No.
Bye, Mom."

To say it's difficult

being the son left behind,

especially when the one who died was the favorite,

is like saying running makes me happy.

Running doesn't just make me happy.

Running keeps me alive.

When I'm running,

the blood pumping through my veins,

the tunes playing in my ears,

the muscles tightening on the inclines,

the problems of the world disappear.

It's just me, the sidewalk, and God.

When I leave the sidewalk

and walk into my house,

it all changes.

Difficult?

Almost impossible.

Daddy was raised

in a house full of women.

Women who did everything for him.

Now I'm left
to do those things
others have done for him
his whole life.

Cook him dinner.
Wash his boxers.
Change his sheets.

He needs me?
I don't think so.

What he needs
is a maid.

Tonight he says,
"Brooklyn, let's get a dog."

I give him a look that says,
Are you crazy?

"What?" he says.
"It'd be great.
You just don't know it
because you've never had one."

That was Mom's fault.
Neat freaks and dogs
don't mix.

And really,
I don't see how
busy girls with enough to take care of
thank-you-very-much
would mix with a dog either.

A maid,
a cook,
and a dog trainer?

I don't think so.

Ma makes a big dish

of ravioli for Gabe's family

along with some bread

and her famous pineapple tiramisu.

Tiramisu means "pick me up" in Italian.

Ma always hopes it will do a little of that.

She took them minestrone soup last week.

When she doesn't know what else to do, she cooks.

She's trying to teach me everything she knows.

I'm the closest thing to the daughter she never had, I guess.

She leaves some ravioli for me and Pop.

We eat in silence.

Too bad there's no tiramisu.

I think we could both use some of that too.

I fall asleep hoping to dream

of Lucca.

Instead I'm standing in the hallway at school.
In the dark.
Alone.

I turn around
and around,
wondering where everyone is.

I want to turn on the lights,
but where do you find the lights
for a school hallway?

There's the faint sound of footsteps.
Someone is far away.
But coming closer.

I listen.
They get louder.

I open my mouth.
I try to speak.
Nothing comes out.

I walk forward,
my arms in front of me,
trying to see my way.

There's a faint light ahead.
I think it's the light to the office.
If I can just make it there,
it'll be okay.

The steps are coming faster.
My pace increases.
Just get to the office.
Nothing can hurt you there.
They'll help you.

The light gets brighter.
I start to run.
Faster and faster
I run,
the beating of my heart
almost as loud
as the pounding of my steps.

I reach the door and look behind me.
I see someone.
Someone's coming.
Right behind me.

I turn the doorknob.
Locked tight.

My fist pounds on the window.
I pound and pound
and open my mouth to scream.

Then, he's there.
In front of me.

Gray skin with eyes
black as the darkest night,
and lips blood red.

He lunges for me
and I scream his name.

"Gabe!"

When I wake up
with my sheets soaked
and sticking to me like bandages,
I can't stop shaking.

Even though I know it was a dream,
something about it
was so much more
than a dream.

A lot more.

#281

Dear Lucca,

I've read six comics. I still can't go back to sleep. I had a horrible dream. I don't even want to talk about it.

Daddy told me after Mom moved out, I could wake him up if I ever needed anything. But then I'd have to tell him about the dream. He'd worry about me. Probably think this thing with Gabe is getting to me. And then who knows what he'd do.

Anyway, what could he do for me, besides give me a hug and tell me to go back to sleep? He can't do anything for me. Not really.

So I guess I'll read about Tom Strong some more. I recently read a review online about him where someone said, "Tom Strong stands for goodness, purity of heart, tolerance, and family." No wonder I like him so much.

Love always,
Brooklyn

Something happened last night

and I am freaking out.

It was almost morning. I was asleep.

I heard a noise.

A scraping noise.

I sat straight up and noticed the window was open, just slightly.

The room was freezing.

I ran to the window and closed it.

I was about to turn on the light, when I felt something.

Like someone was right there.

I lunged for the baseball bat under my bed and started swinging.

I made my way to the light and turned it on.

No one was there.

Nothing was there.

And yet, it was like someone or something *was* there.

And then I heard a whisper.

Not even a whisper.

Something else.

A silent message in my brain.

Make sure Brooklyn is okay.

The curtains fluttered.

A slight shadow emerged on the wall.

And then, he was gone.

The room warmed up.

My goose bumps disappeared.

And I ran out of my room.

Kyra tells me

I look tired.
I tell her I'm fine.
Doing great, in fact.

I don't even tell her
about the nightmare.

That's all it was.
A stupid nightmare.

Although, getting dressed this morning,
I had this odd sense
someone was watching me.

But that's ridiculous.
Gabe is dead.

Dead people don't watch people.
Do they?

I look for Brooklyn

at school

and see her at her locker

talking to Kyra.

She doesn't see me

and I don't stop to talk.

She's fine.

I've seen it for myself.

She's completely fine.

Did I just imagine it?

Whatever "it" was.

I thought someone was there.

I thought I heard the words.

But now, I don't know.

Maybe Ma put something in the ravioli.

That's it.

I'm gonna blame it on the ravioli.

After all, she's fine.

Before I head to bed

Dad gives me a piece of paper
with a website address written on it.

"Check it out," he says.
"It's a shelter here in town.
Some great dogs."

I take it,
knowing I won't look them up.
Knowing my dad just really
doesn't get it.

Lucca told me
he had a dog one time,
when he was younger.
Her name was something silly
like Taffy or Licorice.
I can't remember,
but he said she got hit by a car,
and he never wanted a dog again.

"Man, it hurt when she died," he'd said.
"I didn't want to go through that again."

I've never had a dog.

But I'm pretty sure
I know how he felt.

As I cruise

the Internet,

I sense something behind me.

I turn around, expecting to see

Ma or Pop standing there.

But it's just me.

Or so it seems.

Then I see a shadow pass by

my bedroom window.

It's dark out, except for the soft glow

of the moonlight shining in.

The light seems to change ever so slightly.

I stand and back up toward the door.

What is it?

Who is it?

Am I going completely mad?

I stand there for minutes,

unable to move.

There are noises at my computer.

Tapping noises.

Is that my keyboard—

"Hey!" I yell.

"Lucca, is that you?"

My computer monitor blinks,

and the words

YES HELP BROOKLYN

flash across the screen.

"Lucca?"

Once again

dark hallways
and no one to help me.

I run,
looking for a door outside.
I want out.
Out of this darkness
where the fear inside myself
feels like cement
and I can't run
as fast as I want to.

He's behind me.

Running.
Chasing me.

Breathless,
I try a classroom
doorknob.
When it opens,
I duck inside and search
in the blackness
for a light switch.

But no matter how hard I try,
I can't escape
the darkness.

It consumes me.
It is inside
and outside
and everywhere
I am.

I hide
under the teacher's desk,
my heart beating so loudly,
I'm sure it'll lead him
to me.

And when it does,
there is nowhere else
to go.

It's me
and him
in the darkness.

He moves toward me.
Closer.
And closer.
So close
I can smell the death
that hangs on him
like a comfortable robe.

As his arms reach
under the desk,
I scream
with everything I have.

Screams fill the darkness
and light the way
to a warm bed.

Safe in my warm bed,
crying uncontrollably
not knowing what to do.

And scared I never will.

To: brooklynbaby@sosmail.com
From: nicoferrari@remstat.com
Subj: Need to see you

Hey Brooklyn,

Can we meet? Tomorrow after school?
My house?

Do you like how I end everything with a
question mark?

Let me know. Please! That's a ! not a ? !!

Nico

To: nicoferrari@remstat.com
From: brooklynbaby@sosmail.com
Subj: Re: Need to see you

Hi Nico:

Great to hear from you. Yes, I can meet
you. See you tomorrow.

ttyl
B

Ghosts are only in movies.

Aren't they?

They haunt people or houses,

moaning or carrying chains around,

pissed off about something.

Ghosts don't come to tell you something.

To slip you a message

like it's fifth-period study hall

and there's a party Friday night.

Do they?

So if it is my brother,

here because he's worried

or upset

or something else,

why now?

Why'd he wait until now?

And how am I supposed to feel?

Happy he's back?

Scared of my own brother?

I'll tell you how I feel.

Like I'm cracked in the head,

talking like this.

Ghosts should just stick to movies.

And I should just stick to running.

Too late, though.

Now I'm chasing Brooklyn

because some ghost told me to.

Shit.

Gabe and I

got along.
I liked him.
He liked me.
We were friends.
At least, I thought so.

So why these scary dreams?
Why is he chasing me?

I tell myself
over and over,
he isn't after me.
He's dead.
D-E-A-D.
Dead, dead, dead.

It hate it.
I wish things were different.
But it is what it is.

I gotta move on.
Put it behind me.
Put *him* behind me.
Focus on the good.

If I could figure out
what the good
is, exactly.

#282

Dear Lucca,

Seventh period. Can't focus. Nico wants to see me tomorrow. It's weird. First these nightmares with Gabe, and now Nico's contacting me after all this time?

I really don't want to go. I mean, why should I go? Maybe he's freaking out about Gabe too, and wants to talk about it. Except that I don't want to talk about it! I mean, I don't want to talk about it with anyone but you.

Love always,
Brooklyn

Friday the 13th

Some cities don't have a 13th Street.

Some elevators don't have a 13th floor.

A coven contains 13 witches.

Unlucky?

Maybe.

I've never been superstitious.

But when I realize it's Friday the 13th,

I consider rescheduling with Brooklyn.

The last thing we need is more

bad luck.

But when I get home from school

and find a book magically

pulled from the bookshelf and on my desk,

I decide we better meet up

no matter what date the calendar says.

The book?

A Cry for Help.

What do I know about Nico?

I know he's a senior,
a year older than me.

I know he's got an old, black Toyota pickup
he likes to work on.

I know he likes to cook.
I've had his lasagna and it is to die for.

I know we should have connected sooner.
We might have been able to help each other.

We were probably scared.
Scared to talk about it all.
Scared to see how hurt the other was.
Scared to feel the empty spot Lucca's death has made.

One thing I've learned
is that the empty spot is always there,
no matter who you're with.

I suppose Nico understands that
better than anyone.

I'm watching some trashy TV show

waiting for her to get here.

I'm anxious to talk to her.

See how she's doing.

I remember when I met Brooklyn for the first time.

First thing I thought?

She's hot.

Second thing I thought?

My brother's one lucky dude.

Third thing I thought?

I wonder if they're doing it yet.

My brother worshipped her.

She's artsy. Like him.

He showed me some of her flowery art.

She takes photos of flowers and then draws them.

Beautiful. Like her.

Lucca was an amazing cartoonist.

Drew the funniest characters.

All that talent, gone.

Such a waste.

Since they met in art class,

their first date was a trip to the art museum

and an Italian dinner afterward.

Being Italian, he wanted to see if she liked the food.

Turned out she loved it.

Turned out he loved her.

And the feeling became mutual.

I look out the window and see her

walking up the front path.

Her wavy brown hair is tucked behind her ears

and there's a hint of apprehension in her sad, dark eyes.

She hasn't been here since he died.

I wonder what she's thinking.

I tell myself

it's just a house.

A house with walls,
windows,
doors,
and a roof on top.

I tell myself
don't think about the window
up there on the second floor,
the one he looked out of
while he talked to you on the phone,
telling you how much
he loved you.

I tell myself
don't think about the front door
he walked through a million times
or the welcome mat
that no longer
welcomes him.

I tell myself
don't cry.

But I do.

Because it's
so much more
than just
a house.

Oh no.

She's crying.
I opened the door,
she fell into my arms
and she's standing here crying.
I gently move her to the sofa
in the living room.
What do I do?
I'm not good at this.
I mean, come on.
A crying girl?
In my house?
The one time Ma might actually be useful,
she's not here.
Help!

When he opens the door,

I step in
and an army of memories
comes at me from all sides.

Meeting his parents for the first time.
Studying for finals together, munching on peanut
M&Ms.
Making out in his room when no one was home.

A trickle becomes
a sprinkler.

Nico looks like he wants to call
for a rescue party.

To rescue him.
Not me.

She finally stops crying.

"Sorry," she says. "Just what you needed, right?"

"You want a glass of water?" I ask her.

She nods and follows me to the kitchen.

"Where are your parents?"

"Work."

I feel her eyes on my back

as I fill the glass with ice cubes and water

from the fridge door.

Our eyes meet as I turn around and hand her the glass.

The sadness between us is thick,

like smoke.

I take a deep breath.

She does too.

I watch her swirl the glass around,

the ice cubes

clink

clink

clinking together,

trying to separate

but always coming back together

eventually.

"Why'd you ask me here, Nico?"

"Worried about you, I guess. Are you doing okay?"

She shrugs.

Because she isn't.

But to say it out loud is like admitting defeat.

It's been a year.

We should be okay.

Somewhat okay, anyway.

"Can I see his room?" she asks.

Damn.

This isn't good.

Up the stairs.

Down the hall.
Third door on the right.

The door is closed.

Nico takes a deep breath
before he turns the knob.
Then he turns it
very
very
slowly.

In the movies
the dead person's room
is always so neat,
it's freaky.

This room
is so messy
it's freaky.

An unmade bed,
clothes all over the floor,
dirty dishes on his desk.

It's as if Lucca
was just here this morning,
getting ready for school.

"Oh. My. God."

"Ma wanted to keep it the way he left it."

"Yeah. Obviously."

I walk around
his room,
taking it all in.

His drawings,
on his desk,
and his messy handwriting
scribbled on the pages.

His iPod,
full of songs
he listened to and loved.

His pictures,
me and him,
taped to his computer monitor,
smiling, gushing,
totally in love.

His clothes,
ones he used to wear
on a warm, living body.

I pick a shirt up
off the floor,
and hold it to my face.

Unbelievable.
It's still there.
The slightest scent of Lucca,
the scent of joy, of art, of love,
still there.

I blink fast
trying to keep the tears away
but unable to.

I bury my face
in the shirt
and the tears come
because Lucca
should be sitting at the desk,
listening to his iPod
writing me an e-mail,
wearing this shirt.

He should be here.
And he's not.

The room is suddenly
a merry-go-round,
spinning faster and faster.

My legs buckle beneath me
from the intensity of it all.

Strong, steady arms
wrap around me,
holding me up
and moving me
to the bed,
where we sit down.

I lean into him.

"He should be here, Nico."

He doesn't say anything.
He doesn't have to.

That's why the room
was left
exactly the same.

I let her talk

and cry.

Maybe this is what she needed.

Maybe Lucca was afraid

this Gabe thing might push her over the edge.

Maybe he just wanted me to listen

and tell her it'll be okay.

During the course of our conversation

she says she feels

shocked

sad

confused

terrible

powerless

empty

and bitter

and a couple more I missed.

"I know. It sucks," I tell her.

"But it'll be okay."

She looks at me like I just told her

I have a ghost haunting me.

Like there's no way

that can possibly be true.

I talk and cry

while Nico sits and listens.
Like we've been friends forever.

Finally, I use the shirt
to wipe the tears
and take a deep breath.

We're quiet
for a long time
and then Nico points
to a pair of boxer shorts on the floor.

"I'm glad you picked the shirt."

Before she goes

I ask her if she wants anything.

Something of his to take with her.

"Can I borrow his iPod?"

I nod, so she picks it up and sticks it in her purse.

"I better go," she says. "My dad's going to be looking for dinner soon."

"Does it frequently hide or something?" I ask.

She smiles.

"Lucca was right. You're funny."

I walk her to the door.

She lingers there, her fingers fiddling with the doorknob.

"I still don't get it," she says. "Why get in touch with me now? It's been so long."

Right then, I'm tempted.

Tempted to tell her my brother seems to be haunting me.

But if I want to keep her talking to me,

I can't say that.

So I don't.

"I just had a feeling. A feeling you could use a friend."

I tuck her hair back behind her ear. "And I think I was right."

She looks at me like she wants to tell me something.

But then she looks away, opens the door,

and leaves.

He thought

I might need
a friend.

I'm not exactly sure
what I need
but another friend
probably can't hurt.

The perfect thing

hits my e-mail at just the right time.

A sprint triathlon coming up in the next town over.

I click the register button

and dream of losing myself

in the intense training

that will ensue

in the coming days and weeks.

I'll lose myself in the pain.

It might not make sense.

But it works.

Half his iPod

is filled with
The Killers
because he loved them.

There's some
Fall Out Boy,
Linkin Park,
Coldplay,
and All-American Rejects
and it's like
I'm in Lucca's head,
being Lucca,
listening to the music
he loved.

The beautiful thing is,
music can be like
a time machine.

One song—
the lyrics, the melody, the mood—
can take you back
to a moment in time
like nothing else can.

And so,
when the song comes up
that takes me back
to a night
in a hot, sweaty gym
where we danced slow
for the first time,
I close my eyes,
listen to *You and Me*
by Lifehouse
and it's like I'm there.

I'm there and
we're dancing.
I look up at him,
he kisses me,
the room is glowing,
my heart is pounding,
my head is screaming
I love you, Lucca!

Music is so personal.

I fall asleep
with the music playing.

It comforts me.
Like he's lying
right there next to me,
his breath,
the sweetest music of all,
whispering in my ear.

I wake up freezing.

The window is open again.

I go to close it and when I do,

I see something written on the glass.

It's faint,

like someone wrote it with a dirty fingertip,

but if I squint my eyes just right

I can see the words.

help her

I spin around and look for any other signs

that he was here.

Nothing.

I don't get it.

I wish he would tell me how exactly

I'm supposed to help her!

I'm in a field.

A big, open field
filled with beautiful white daisies.

In the distance,
a forest stands at attention.

I'll stay here,
feeling sparkly and new,
like laundry hung out to dry
on a warm, sunny day.

It's peaceful here.
Serene.
It feels like we belong together,
me and these daisies.

But then,
something moves
in the distance,
near the forest.

I feel panic
rise up in me.

Has he found me again?
Am I in danger
no matter where I go?

As the figure approaches,
I see that it's him.

He's getting closer,
and I urge my legs
to start moving.

A breeze picks up
and I watch as the
precious, fragile flowers
blow in the wind,
their stems reaching up,
offering me hundreds
of helping hands.

I run through the field,
crushing their helping hands
like a cold, heartless soul.

I run,
knowing they can't help me.

I wake up,
feeling like no one can.

#283

Dear Lucca,

*I feel like you're the only one I can talk to
about this. About Gabe. About these frightening
nightmares that are more real than any dreams
I've ever had. Why is this happening?*

*Why aren't you visiting me in my dreams?
Why him? I don't get it. It makes no sense.*

Please, help me. I need it to make sense.

*Love always,
Brooklyn*

I'm not really good

at detective work.

Look for clues,

narrow down possibilities,

follow hunches,

identify leads.

I want to know

where to go

and what to do.

Give me a list

with specific things to do,

and I'm good to go.

Otherwise, forget it.

I write a note and tape it to my window—

I'M NOT A DETECTIVE.

BE SPECIFIC!

I spend the day

by myself,
just walking.

Walking around town
looking in windows
filled with pretty things.

They call it
window shopping.

I call it
window dreaming.

Dreaming of being
the mannequin
smiling,
looking hot,
nothing wrong,
the world
picture perfect
from the window.

Another Saturday.

Another long run,

hoping to put distance

between me

and everything else.

The farther,

the better.

Only problem is,

the distance is just temporary,

Because no matter how far I go,

I always have to come back.

A dark, narrow street

void of houses
or buildings
or people.

No matter how fast I run,
how hot I get,
how hard I try to lose him,
he's behind me.

His footsteps now
more familiar to me
than my own voice.

Like a soldier at war,
being chased by the enemy,
I search for places to hide.
But there aren't any.

So I
just
keep
running.

Then, suddenly,
like an unexpected break
in the storm,
the footsteps stop.

I glance behind me,
and there's nothing to see.

I stop
and breathe
a sigh of relief.

Until I look
in front of me.
He's there.
Right
there.

"Fear controls you," he tells me.
In that moment
my heart is
a ticking bomb,
ready to explode.

I will myself awake,
gasping for breath,
feeling like I ran for miles
even if I was in my bed
all night long.

Spaghetti Sunday

is my favorite day of the month.

The third Sunday of every month,

Ma makes a big batch of spaghetti with meatballs,

and relatives fill our house like fish fill a net

on a good fishing day.

The guys eat and watch football or basketball or baseball,

depending on the season,

while the girls eat

and talk births or weddings or funerals

depending on the month.

Ma's spaghetti slid into Lucca's heart as a toddler

and never left.

I know when she makes it,

she thinks of him,

how he'd come in and ask for a sample of sauce

as it simmered on the stove.

She'd fill a wooden spoon just for him.

He'd slurp the sauce.

She'd reach up and wipe his chin.

He'd say, "Perfection, Ma."

She'd smile, looking at him, and say, "Yes. It is."

I always wondered,

did he know she wasn't talking

about the sauce?

After I go

to the comic book store,
Kyra and I meet up
at the movies
to escape life
and death
for a couple of hours.

We always get there early
to sit in the way-back,
where the seats are roomy
and our whispers are safe.

The box of Junior Mints
passes between us,
keeping time with our words.

She tells me about this new guy, Tyler,
who's in her English class
and how he has eyes
the color of sea glass
and hair the color of sand.

"Maybe he's a merman," I tell her.

"Well, he can take me under the sea any day," she says.

With eyes as bright and warm
as a sunflower
and smooth, dark skin,
Kyra is by far the prettiest girl in our class.

I don't know if boys are intimidated by her
or afraid of her or what,
but I know her heart is open and ready
for a special guy to walk in.

She's telling me more about her merman
when we see Gabe's sister, Audrey,
and two of her friends walk in.

They take their seats.
Audrey sits quietly
while her friends chat and laugh.

Kyra and I exchange a look
without words,
and we know our minds
have traveled to the same place together.

The lights dim,
while anticipation rises.

I hope the movie is spectacular.

Because for some people,
it's not quite so easy
to escape life
and death.

My cousin Michael

gets my attention from across the room

of noodle heads and waves me outside.

Michael goes to a different school.

"What happened with Gabe?" he asks.

I shrug. "He's dead."

"But how?"

"Drugs," I say, like it's so simple,

which of course it's anything but.

"It blows," he says. "You okay?"

"Yeah. I was pissed for a while.

But I'm trying to get over it."

I grab the football from the lawn

and motion to him to go long.

"Nico. Seriously. Are you okay?"

Concern covers his face like a ski mask.

I smile.

"I'm fine, Michael. I even signed up for a sprint triathlon.

Now I just need to start training."

"By yourself?" he asks.

"Unless you want to do it with me," I say.

The ball spirals toward him

and falls into his arms

like it belongs there.

"No way," he says. "Not my idea of fun."

It may not be fun all the time.

But it's better than thinking about

dead people.

I watch the merman

from afar.

He floats around the library,
waves of eyes
watching him as he goes.

There's something about him.
Something that captures
your attention and holds it
like a beacon at night
in the strongest of storms.

What is it?
What is it about him?

When he suddenly turns
and his sea-green eyes meet mine,
in that instant
it's like my toes hit the
cold Pacific ocean,
and I know.

He is not *of* the ocean.
He *is* the ocean.

A sea of life
full of all things mysterious
and beautiful
and alive.

What a wondrous thing to be.

#284

Dear Lucca,

Remember how we talked about going to the beach together? We planned to go in the summer, when it was warm. I wanted to walk along the beach with you, holding hands, our bare feet making footprints until the waves quietly washed them away.

I loved dreaming with you. Making plans with you. We had things to do, places to go, things to see.

Now there's no more plans for me. So, I'll just sit here, dreaming of the cool, blue ocean. And you. When I'm daydreaming, I always dream of you.

Love always,
Brooklyn

My talk with Brooklyn

last week doesn't seem to be enough.

All weekend,

A Cry for Help

made the rounds in my room.

Every time I entered,

the book was somewhere new.

On my pillow.

In my sock drawer.

Between my old Little League trophies.

Tired of the game,

I threw it in the trash can.

Outside.

As I sit in class,

I think back to this morning.

I woke up

to the loud, angry noises

of the garbage trucks on the street.

I woke up

to goose bumps all over my body.

I woke up

to my hand gripping a book.

A Cry for Help.

I know what I'll find

when I get home.

Daddy on the sofa
with his feet on the coffee table,
the newspaper in his hands
and the TV turned to ESPN.

I know
what we'll talk about
while I make dinner.

He'll ask about my day
and I'll say it was fine
and then he'll tell me about
some of the animals he helped
at his veterinarian practice.

I know
what will happen
during dinner.

We'll watch TV
until I get up and take our dishes
to the dishwasher.

Then I'll go to my room
and supposedly do homework,
which I sometimes do,
and sometimes don't.

I know
what will happen
when it's time to go to bed.

He'll say, "I love you, angel.
Sweet dreams."

I'll say, "I love you, too"
all the while thinking,

Why'd you make them go?

Over dinner

Ma asks me if I've seen Audrey at school.

"Yeah. A few times."

"Does she look okay?" Ma asks.

I shrug. "Looks fine to me.

Hanging out with her friends. Like usual."

Pop nods. "She's a strong girl. She'll get through this."

"That's what we thought about Gabe," Ma says softly.

And she's exactly right.

Later in my room, I think about that.

And I think about Brooklyn and how

I thought she just needed a shoulder to cry on.

But maybe she needs more.

Maybe she can't put out a call for help,

so Lucca's doing it for her.

I start to call her.

And then I stop.

Because it's so bizarre.

I can't just call her out of nowhere

and tell her I think she needs help.

I mean, what the hell does that sound like?

I'm pretty sure it sounds like

she'll hang up on my ass.

Over dinner

Dad tells me
about an old cocker spaniel
named Barnaby
who died today.

He was old and sick,
blind and going deaf,
and his owner
wanted to give him
peace.

I say, "See. That's exactly why I don't want a dog."

"Why?"

"Because it'll just die."

"Everybody dies, Brooklyn."

Like that makes it okay or something.

Pop's been on my back

like a hump on a camel

about getting a job again.

I worked over the summer

as a waiter and when my

fall course load was heavy, I quit.

Couldn't stand the whining customers—

the meat's too red

the gravy too cold

the cake too rich.

Won't be doing that again anytime soon.

I'd get a job as a grease monkey if I could,

except they have guys

with years of experience under their hoods

lining up for work, and what have I got?

What kind of dressing would you like on your salad, ma'am?

As if that's going to help me.

Anyway, I really don't want to work.

I just want to run.

Wish I got paid for doing that.

Running's my kind of work.

Mom calls to talk

and when we're caught up
on her and the twins,
she asks
about school,
about Kyra,
about my art.

Art?
Color?
Beauty?

They're all foreign to me.
As foreign as the Taj Mahal.

That which used to be
a drawing table
is now a
dirty clothes receptacle.

Apparently, I'm
airing my dirty laundry
in the truest sense
of the words.

To: brooklynbaby@sosmail.com
From: nicoferrari@remstat.com
Subj: Just checking

Brooklyn,

Everything going okay? Just wanted you
to know, if you ever need anything, don't
be afraid to ask. Anything at all . . .

Nico

While Mr. Ingalls

drones on in Algebra 2,
I sit in a bathroom stall,
drawing a rose on the wall.

Bathroom art is all about
killing time and nothing else.

Two girls come in,
talking about a party
Friday night.

I draw the last leaf
and go out,
wanting to see who they are.

Melinda and Bree,
two of the biggest
stoners in school.

"Hey," I say.

They both return the greeting
while I approach the sink.

"You and Gabe were friends, right?" Bree asks.
I nod.

They look at each other,
then back at me.
I focus on the soap
lathering in my hands.
I know they're trying to decide
what to say.
Perhaps how much to say.

"There's a party Friday night," Melinda says.
"At Ben's house. You should come."

"It's to honor Gabe," Bree says.
"The band's gonna play.
It'll be good. You know?"

I turn the water off
and reach for a paper towel.

"Thanks," I tell them.
"I'll think about it."

They smile, then turn back
to each other and whatever
business they have
in the bathroom
together.

A party.
To honor him.
Interesting idea.

A Cry for Help

is on my pillow again,

like a good-night chocolate,

but not quite as sweet.

Okay.

I get it.

You're obviously trying to tell me something.

When I take the book to my desk,

I hear music.

My computer is playing a CD.

The song?

Fix You by Coldplay.

"I'll talk to her tomorrow, Lucca," I whisper.

"I promise."

I'm swimming

in the light, bright ocean
under the waves,
with hundreds of
vibrantly colored fish
all around me.

The colors are more vivid
than anything I've seen
in a dream before.

I swim slowly with the fish,
tranquility gently
guiding us along.

Until the sea darkens.
The fish scatter.
And I'm alone.

No footsteps to hear.
No desks to hide under.
No streets or fields to run in.

I know he's coming.
And only then do my lungs
fill with water,
and I scramble to the surface.

There, I gasp for breath,
scanning the vast sea of blue.

He isn't far at all.

I swim as hard as I can.
But it isn't hard enough.

Soon I'm pulled
down
down,
down,
choking,
gagging,
unable to breathe.

When I force myself awake,
the blankets are
completely twisted
around me.

Like a mermaid tangled
in strands of seaweed.

As I untangle myself,
I notice the clock says 5:30.
It's early, but I think of the e-mail
and grab my phone.

When he answers,
it's as if I'm still
underwater.

I can hardly breathe.
Or speak.

I'm on my way

to the pool to do laps

when the phone rings.

I see her name and press TALK.

"Hey, Brooklyn. It's early. You okay?"

Silence.

"Brooklyn?"

More silence.

"Okay, I'm coming over.

Go out front and wait for me."

Suddenly, silence scares me

more than any ghost could.

The cold morning air
makes me
s
h
i
v
e
r
and s h a k e.

My eyes scan the dark street,
like a dog keeping watch,
and I half expect Gabe
to come running toward me.

I resist the urge
to retreat inside
to the warmth and safety
of home.

Nico pulls up
a minute later.

I get in,
and only then do I realize
how scary I must look,
with my bed-head hair
and my dad's extra-large raincoat
thrown over me.

His car is warm,
but his voice
is what soothes me.

"Brooklyn, what happened?"

I try to blink back the tears
but I can't,
and so they fall.

He reaches over
and pulls me to him,
hushing me like a small child
who's had a nightmare.

If only he knew.

This girl

is a faucet with legs.

She's crying.

Again.

Obviously, my brother is right.

She needs help.

But what kind of help?

And why am I the one who's supposed to give it?

She calms down fairly quickly

as I hold her close and let her know

it's going to be okay.

When I ask her what's wrong, she doesn't say.

I ask again and again,

begging like a blind man on the street corner.

Finally she says,

"I just feel so . . . alone."

There's more though.

She's hiding something.

How can I get the real reason to come out and play?

She kicks my duffel bag at her feet.

"Where were you going so early?" she asks.

"The pool," I tell her. "I'm training for a sprint triathlon."

"What's that?" she asks.

"A half-mile swim. Twelve-mile bike. Three-mile run."

She looks confused. "You can't be serious."

"I am. It's not that hard. I mean, if you train right.

Honestly, it helps me. To deal with it all."

And as I relay this information to her,

a brilliant idea strikes at the perfect time.

Running helps me.

Maybe it can help her.

"You should do it with me," I say.

"We can train together. It'd be good for you!"

She looks at me like I've asked her to join the marines.

"No. Oh, no. I have school. And my dad.

I mean, no. I don't think I could.

Besides, I haven't been sleeping well."

"Brooklyn, it's great for that.

You'll sleep better if you work out."

There's something in her eyes that

tells me she wants to believe me.

She turns and stares down the dark, quiet street.

I wish I could hear her thoughts.

I wish I could make her feel safe enough to tell me.

I wish I could get her to say yes.

He wants me

to do what?

Swim
and bike
and run
all in one race?

Is he crazy?

He thinks I could do that?

I'm an artist
not an athlete.

Except lately,
I'm not much
of anything.

I look at him.
Strong.
Happy.
Excited.

I can't even remember
what that feels like.

I'm so tired of
thinking about Gabe,
worrying about Gabe,
running from Gabe.

Maybe some distraction
is just what I need.

Nico's still staring at me,
willing me to say okay.

And to my surprise,
that's exactly what I say.

I watch her

go back inside and wonder
what's really going on.
She never said.
At least we're making progress.
Going somewhere instead of
standing still.
Motion is always preferable
to stagnation.
When you move,
things happen.
You're alive.
Stay still too long,
and it's hard to get moving again.
Gotta keep things moving.

When I get to school,

I start to tell Kyra
I'm having a hard time.

But her eyes glimmer
like diamonds in a glass case
as she talks about Tyler.

They're working together
on a project in class,
getting to know each other
and apparently,
there are sparks.

I can't douse those sparks.
Sparks are good
because they lead to fire.
Warm, lovely fire.

If I could just figure out
what Gabe wants.

Fear controls me?
What did he mean?

"Brooklyn?"
Kyra grabs my hand.
"You okay?"

I look into her sparkly eyes.
I give her my best smile.
"Yeah. Of course! I'm great!"

#285

Dear Lucca,

*Do you remember when we were falling in love?
When we couldn't stand to be apart for any
length of time? I loved that feeling. I loved knowing
you'd be waiting for me before and after school,
in between classes, and lunchtime. I loved having
something to look forward to each day.*

*Maybe that's why I've agreed to do this crazy
thing with your brother. I think it's about needing
something to look forward to. I may hate it, I may
love it, but at least it's something to get out of bed
for every day.*

*Love always,
Brooklyn*

I still can't believe

she said she'd do it.

I told her all she needs is

the right attitude and dedication.

She called last night

to tell me she went to the website

and signed up.

We're meeting this morning to run.

Lucca would be so proud of her.

He didn't visit last night

so maybe I'm heading in the right direction.

When I pull into the parking lot

and see her running around the track,

I know I am.

My first day of training

goes something like
jog two laps,
walk one,
jog two,
walk two,
jog one,
walk one.

When we're finished,
we make plans
for the next few days.

During the school week,
we'll meet in the mornings,
before school.

On the weekends,
we'll do more,
varying what we do
and for how long.

As we talk,
I can't believe
I'm really doing it.

Some people
look at my flower art
and think it's so amazing
I'm able to do *that*.

It isn't amazing to me.
It's just color and paper
and trying my best to do the beauty
of the flowers
justice.

But an athlete,
who can push himself to go on
when his body is
longing,
pleading,
crying
to stop?

That's amazing.

Nico says the race will be a piece of cake
as long as we're consistent.

It's like
if you consistently say thanks,
being grateful is easy.

If you consistently say I love you,
being loving is easy.

If I consistently train,
being a triathlete will be easy.

I'll believe it when I see it.

"Good job,"

I tell her as we walk to our cars.

"That wasn't too hard," she says.

"It'll get harder, right?"

"The key is to be consistent," I tell her.

"Consistently train, consistently push yourself,

and the race will be a piece of cake."

"Mmmm, cake," she says. "I'm hungry."

I smile. Look at my watch.

"Just enough time to shower and grab some breakfast."

We talk some more about the coming days

and what I have planned for training.

She listens, nods her head, not saying much,

and again I wish I knew what she was thinking.

Sometimes she's hard to read.

Finally, she speaks.

"This working out stuff, it really helps you?"

"Yeah," I reply. "It helps. A lot."

"Good. Okay. See you tomorrow morning, then.

Wait, tomorrow's Friday, right?"

"Right."

"Listen to this. I got invited to a party tomorrow night.

Bree and Melinda. Apparently it's a party to honor Gabe.

You heard about it?"

I shake my head. "But hey, you're an athlete now.

Athletes don't party."

She waves her hand at me and walks away. "Don't worry."

Kind of hard not to.

I'm back home

and showered before Daddy
even wakes up.

Later, we meet in the kitchen,
as the coffeemaker
gurgles and spits,
the delicious aroma
circling around us.

I'm making toast
when the phone rings.
He answers it,
while I spread peanut butter.

The coffeemaker stops,
so I get two cups and fill them up.
When he comes back,
he's got a scowl on his face
that screams trouble.

"What?" I ask. "What is it?"

"It was your math teacher.
Apparently you're flunking."

I gulp. "It's fine, Daddy.
Please don't worry.
I'll bring it up.
I've just gotten a little behind.
That's all."

"A little behind?" he says.
"An F is not a little behind.
Should I get you a tutor?"

I shake my head. "No. I don't need one.
I'll catch up. I promise."

He grabs his cup off the counter
and takes a big swig.

"I'm giving you a month," he says.
"Understand?"

I nod.
And then he stomps out.

Maybe training
will help my grades, too.
It seems to be the solution
to everything else.

#286

Dear Lucca,

Life is so freaking hard. How do people do it? How do people get up every day and deal with the shit?

It really makes you understand why there are so many messed-up people in the world. I mean, it's tough, trying to deal with demands coming at you from all sides.

Unless you're Tom Strong. Then, you can handle anything.

If you could have one superhero power, what would it be? I'd want the ability to be invisible. Maybe then, everyone would just leave me alone.

Love always,
Brooklyn

At lunchtime

Brooklyn's in the caf

sitting with a group of girls.

I wave, and she smiles at me.

I grab my usual fare of chips and beef jerky

and head to my truck.

I haven't eaten lunch anywhere else in so long.

I have friends.

Or I think I have friends.

Since my brother died, they act strange.

Or maybe I act strange.

Every day, I pull out my sword,

a warrior ready to battle life,

and do what I have to do to survive the pain

of living without Lucca.

He was my best friend.

My very best friend.

So excuse me if I act strange.

Losing your brother and your best friend

all in one fell swoop

will do that to a guy.

My friends

are hungry like wolves
at lunchtime.

But not for the
taco salads
they nibble on
as they talk.

Hungry for love.

Elizabeth's gaga over a guy named Gavin,
who sits next to her in Art class.
I've seen her blinking big puppy-dog eyes
and wagging her bootylicious tail,
trying to get his attention.

Kyra's talking about her merman,
wiggling in her seat like a two-year-old.

"Please go to the dance with me next week," she says.
"I heard Tyler talking to one of his friends.
He's planning on going.
Please, Brooklyn?"

I sigh. "Maybe."

They're hungry all right.

As for me,
I eat my taco salad,
wondering if I'll
ever feel hungry
again.

This morning

we meet at the pool,

the stars and the moon our only spectators.

When she pulls up in her dad's Mercedes,

with DOG DOC on the vanity plates,

I walk over with two cups of steaming hot coffee

and hand her one.

She smiles and says, "Thanks."

"Much better," I say.

"What?" she asks.

"A smile. Instead of tears."

She nods. "Yeah. It is."

Did he really bring me

coffee?

Fortunately, the caffeine
isn't all that necessary
this morning.

I slept really well last night.
No dreams.
Thank God, no dreams.
Today, I feel good.

As we're walking inside,
I say, "Thanks again, Nico.
That was really nice of you."

He smiles his million-dollar smile.
"You're welcome."

He *is* nice.

And I can't help but think,
just like his brother.

We swim for a while

then I get out to watch her.

I'm relieved she's a strong swimmer.

It can be the trickiest part of the race.

Her strokes are as smooth

as the coffee we just drank

I give her a few tips on knowing

when and how often to take breaths.

She glides through the water,

adjusting her breaths like I told her.

Perfect.

Absolutely perfect.

In the pool

the water washes
over me and inside
my worries
about Lucca,
about Gabe,
about my family,
about school
about life
wash
away.

Some mothers
do their birthing
in water.

Some patients
do their therapy
in water.

Some children
do their playing
in water.

It   is   gentle.
It   is   soothing.
It   is   forgiving.

It   is   just what I needed

                                    today.

On our way out,

I say, "Brooklyn, about that party—"

"Don't worry," she says. "I'm not going.

I won't lie. I thought about it."

She looks at me and smiles.

I love the way her eyes crinkle when she smiles.

"Tuesday, when they asked me?" she says.

"I wanted to go. Maybe even yesterday,

I wanted to go.

But now, right now, in this moment,

after that awesome workout?

I don't want to go.

And I can't wait for tomorrow, Nico.

See you then."

She walks away and I breathe

a big, heavy, deep

sigh of relief.

After dinner,

listening to the *Joy, Not Sorrow* CD,
I'm safe in the lair
that is my room.

The place
I've always felt safest.

Where it's just me
and my thoughts
and my letters to Lucca.

Safe, that is,
until *he* visits me
outside of my dreams.

Sitting in my chair,
writing in my notebook,
a cold, invisible feather
tickles my cheek.

A soft brush
of whispers
strokes my hair.

There is nothing to see.
Nothing to hear.
But I know with all my being
Gabe is with me
in my lair.

And I have to wonder,
is this God's way
of kicking me out?

#287

Dear Lucca,

*I hate this. What have I done to deserve this? I
don't know.*

*But I feel so alone and like there will be no end to
this madness. I mean, how does it all end?*

*Love always,
Brooklyn*

Something urges me

to go.

A feeling.

A hunch.

A voice that says, "She's there."

Even if she said this morning

she wouldn't go, things change.

Sunny one minute, pouring the next,

we're all like Mother Nature

when it comes right down to it.

So I make some calls,

find out where the party is, and I go.

I spot her dad's car, parked on the street,

a head behind the wheel.

I knock on the window and she rolls it down.

Tears are streaming down her face.

"What are you doing here, Brooklyn?" I ask.

She shakes her head, her face filled with sadness,

it actually pains me to look at it.

"I don't know," she whispers.

I open the door and pull her to her feet.

She reaches up and grabs hold of me,

and so we stand there, just holding each other.

Sunny one minute.

Pouring the next.

"I'm going for a run,"
I tell my dad.

"A run? When did that start?"

"Last week.
Just trying something different."

"You know, a dog would be
something different," he says.

It makes me smile.
Can't blame the guy for trying.

When I see Nico at the track,
he doesn't say anything about last night,
and I'm glad for that.
I don't know what happened.
Looking for something
in the wrong place, I guess.

At least it was another night
of no dreams.

I run faster.

Gotta make sure
I'm good and tired tonight.

We're running the track

and I can't help but think

it feels like

she's running from something.

Or someone.

I glance behind us.

But of course, nothing's there.

After all,

aren't the scariest things in life

those things you can't see?

As we walk to our cars,

I ask Nico, "What was the name of your dog?"

"Wow," he says. "That's random."

"My dad's been wanting to get one.
And I was thinking about Lucca.
How he said he never wanted another one."

He nods.
Looks up at the sky as we hear a rumble.

"His name was Oreo."

Right.
Not candy.
A cookie.

"What about you?" I ask him.
"Would you ever get another dog?"

We stand by his truck.
Raindrops start to fall,
and I watch as they dance
on the pavement.

"I wanted to get another one.
Lucca didn't. So, we didn't."

"You could get one now," I say.

As soon as I say it, I regret it.
Like he'd rather have a dog
than his brother.

He reaches for the door handle,
ready to take cover from the rain.
Or my stupid comment.

"See ya later, Brooklyn."

I wave and walk to my car,
kicking myself the whole way.

I stop at the park again

and swing.

Slow at first.

Then higher and higher.

Back and forth.

I close my eyes and let the rain

pelt my face.

Back and forth.

I'm glad for the rain.

Back and forth.

It's good camouflage.

I stay up

until my head literally hurts
I'm so tired.

I go to bed with
Lucca's music
softly playing in my ears.

I tell myself it will protect me.
He will protect me.

Wherever you are, Lucca.
Please.
Protect me.

Pop asks me over breakfast

how the job search is going.

"Not a lot out there right now," I tell him.

"Maybe when summer comes and I have more time."

"Well, you sure have a lot of time to work out," he says.

Pisses. Me. Off.

He never would have told Lucca,

You sure have a lot of time to draw.

He could do no wrong.

I, on the other hand,

can apparently do no right.

I wake up refreshed

and ready for the day.
Nico's taking me
on a long bike ride.

I look outside,
happy to see the
clear sky and sunshine
after yesterday's storm
has passed.

It'll be chilly,
but it won't be wet.

So far, I love working out.
It's only been a few days,
and sure, things could change.
But I love it.

And I realize,
it's been a really long time
since I've said that
about anything.

"Look at that sky," she says.

"Have you ever seen a sky as bright as that?"

I hadn't noticed anything,

thinking too much about where we're going,

how far, and if we have everything we need.

I take a second to look up,

shading my eyes from the piercing sun.

"Dazzling," I say, trying to be funny.

Then I wonder, how long has it been

since I actually looked at the sky?

We ride our bikes through the city,

to the road that heads toward the beach.

We won't go quite that far.

But here, on this road,

we can stretch out and ride.

Here, on this road,

we can feel the sun on our skin

and smile.

Here, on this road,

it feels like maybe,

just maybe

everything will be okay.

When we find a spot

to stop for water
and a PowerBar,
I can't help but notice
how relaxed Nico looks.

Riding definitely suits him.

We sit in the tall grass,
far enough back,
no one from the road
can even see us.

It feels like a place
you can safely
share secrets.

"Do you ever get scared, Nico?"

"Yeah. Of course."

"What scares you?" I ask.

He lies down in the grass
and closes his eyes,
the sun his blanket.

"You mean besides big snakes?"

I laugh. "Yeah. Besides that."

"Besides eating the school's turkey pot pie?"

"Yes. Besides that, too."

The breeze blows, ruffling the grass,
and I almost don't hear him when he whispers,
"I'm afraid I can't help you."

The honesty in that reply
takes my breath away.

"What do you mean?"

she asks me.

And I could tell her.

Right here, I could tell her

my brother's been haunting me,

because he's worried about her

and now I'm worried about her

and I just want to know what's going on.

"Are you doing okay?" is all I can manage.

"I just get . . . worried sometimes."

"Yeah," she says. "I'm okay.

I mean, as okay as I can be.

It's been a hard year. You know that."

He sits up.

"You scared me Friday night," I tell her.

"Want to talk about it?"

She shakes her head no.

And suddenly there's this awkwardness

that wasn't there before.

"We better head back," she says.

"Yeah. You're probably right.

Ma will kill me if I'm late for dinner."

I stand up, reach my hand down,

and she takes it, so I can help her to her feet.

As I start to walk toward the bikes,

she grabs my arm and says,

"Nico. Thank you.

For letting me do this race with you.

It is helping me.

You are helping me."

Man, I hope she's right.

I'm tired.

But there's laundry,
grocery shopping,
dinner,
and homework
all needing to be done.

At least Daddy helps me with the
grocery shopping.

"Let's just grab burgers for dinner," he says
on our way home from the store.

We head to his favorite burger place
and as we do,
we pass by Another Galaxy.

My mind starts racing.
It's Sunday.
I didn't go today.
My heart pounds.

"Dad," I say. "What time is it?"

"Six thirty. Why?"

Crap. It's closed.
It closes at 6:00 on Sundays.

"I, just, I wanted to go to Another Galaxy."

He laughs. "You have enough comics to read.
You have a whole box, right?"

That's not the point.
It's our thing, Daddy.
It's always been our thing.

Ma asks me

to help her make baked ziti for dinner.

She hands me one of her aprons.

"I don't need it, Ma."

Her eyes narrow.

Like cooking without an apron

is worse than riding a motorcycle

without a helmet.

"Fine," she says. "Do it your way."

I sigh and grab it from her.

"I can never do anything right, can I?"

Now she sighs. A long, tired sigh.

"Nico, that's not true.

You're a good boy. We love you, son.

You know that. Don't you?"

She reaches up and gives my chin a slight squeeze.

I nod.

And then I put on the apron.

Kyra sees me

talking to Nico
as we make our workout plan
for the week.

We took the morning off,
but tomorrow, it's back to it.

"What are you guys doing?" she asks
after he leaves.

"Training together."

"Is that all?" she asks,
her eyebrow raised.

"Yes, Kyra.
That's all."

"It's okay."

"What's okay?" I ask.

"Just, you know,
whatever happens, it's okay.
Don't be afraid."

And I think,
what a weird thing
to say.

I feel eyes on us

in the hallway as we talk.
Like talking to someone
means something more
than just talking.
Jesus.
Like she would ever want
anything to do with me
after she had the greatest boyfriend
in the history of mankind.
Talking is just talking, people.
Get a grip.

I'm in a castle,

standing in a tower,
looking down through a window
at the beautiful garden,
the sun setting in the distance.

The beauty in the moment
brings tears to my eyes.

Sky blue pink,
the backdrop for
roses in every color
blooming in the garden.

When Lucca
comes running up the walkway,
beside the gardens,
I gasp.

His eyes scan the area,
as if looking for someone.

"Lucca," I yell, waving.
"Lucca, I'm up here!

He comes closer to the tower,
still looking around him.

"Brooklyn, don't be afraid," he yells.

"Afraid?" I say, laughing.
"I'm not afraid of you."

"It's not about me," he said.

"Please, Lucca, come up here.
Come and see me.
Please?"

He shakes his head
and looks around some more.
"I can't.
I'm not supposed to be here.
Remember what I said, okay?"

In an instant,
he's gone.
Not the first time.

My heart breaks.
Also not the first time.

I long to go after him.
To find him
and hold him
and kiss him
in the loveliest of gardens.

Behind me,
I hear a noise
and when I turn,
there's Gabe,
standing in front of
the only exit.

"No," I say.
"Please, no."

"Stop the fear," he says,
his eyes fierce.
He takes a step toward me.
And another.

"Please," I say,
backing toward the window.
"Leave me alone."

He's just a step away now.

The window's here,
my only way out.

I don't hesitate.

I

jump.

For hours after that,
I'm awake,
writing in my notebook
and reading comic books.

The last time I look at the clock,
it says 4:30.
Finally, I feel tired.
Like I can sleep.
My alarm will go off at 5:00.
I wonder
if I'll hear it. . . .

#288

Dear Lucca,

*I can't believe it. You were there in my dream.
For only a second, but it was you. I loved seeing
you. You said you weren't supposed to be there.
What does that mean? Of course you should be
in my dreams. You more than anyone should
be in my dreams. Don't say things like that.*

*I'd actually hoped I was done with those dreams.
But I guess not. Why can't he just leave me alone?*

*Anyway, if I'm going to keep dreaming, I hope
you come back.*

*Love always,
Brooklyn*

She doesn't show up

at the swimming pool.

Maybe she forgot.

Maybe she went to the track instead.

I swim alone,

trying to block out the other maybes

popping up in my brain.

The ones that make me want to climb out,

drive to her house,

and make sure she's okay.

Maybe she overslept.

That's got to be it.

She just overslept.

At lunch, I wander outside,

needing fresh air in my lungs
more than greasy food in my stomach.

Kyra's in the library
studying for a test.

I see Nico,
or part of him anyway,
sticking out of the hood of his truck,
like a skilled lion-tamer
in his lion's mouth.

"Hey," I say.
"Nice engine."

He stands up and gives me a look,
as if I've just told him
he has a nice ass.

A little taken aback.

"You know a nice engine when you see it?"

"Not really," I tell him.
"Just thought it sounded good."

He walks to the cab
and grabs a quart of oil.
"Where were you this morning?"

"Rough night.
Didn't sleep well.
Sorry."

I let out a deep breath
as he puts the oil in.

"I wish life was like a car engine," I say.

His eyes squint
in confusion.

"When something's wrong," I explain,
"you get a mechanic, and it's fixed."

He stands up. Looks at me.
"Is something wrong, Brooklyn?"

I shrug and turn my face
toward the shining sun,
wanting it to shine forever,
keeping the darkness at bay.

"It's a lot of things, I guess.
Mostly, I just wish we could go back.
I miss him, you know?"

"Yeah," he says. "I know."

"I better go.
See ya, Nico."

"Brooklyn?"

I turn around.

He's smiling.
I feel warmth.
Is that the sun?
Is that a dimple on his left cheek?

"I'm a pretty good mechanic.
Just keep that in mind, okay?"

I can fix cars.

I can fix fences.

I can even fix a drippy faucet.

But if this is a broken-heart issue

and Lucca is relying on me to fix that,

I don't know if I'm the right guy.

I've never fixed a single

broken heart in my whole life.

Been the one to do the breaking

a time or two.

But fix one?

Whole new territory.

I sleep well

for hours,
until rancid breath
on my face
wakens me.

Fear creeps down my spine
and I gasp, sitting up.

I wait
and watch.

What does he want?
Will he ever tell me?
Or is he just tormenting me
for the fun of it?

Out of the corner of my eye
I see something move.

A little white moth
flying here and there,
around my lamp,
seeking the light
like a lost child
seeking his mother.

And then,
in an instant,
the moth disappears.

Gone.

Until it miraculously
appears from nowhere
dropped on my blankets
right in front of me.

Dead.

Last night

I had a dream.

Lucca and I sitting in a baseball stadium,

the only ones in the stands,

with the field spread out before us like a feast for a king.

Baseball hats on our heads.

Blue sky and warm sunshine.

The smell of hot dogs in the air.

Two brothers, side by side, waiting for the game to start.

"Who's playing?" I asked.

"Does it matter?" he asked.

"No. Not really."

Me and him together, that's what mattered.

"Brooklyn misses you," I said.

He looked at me, his blue eyes stern.

"It doesn't matter. You're there. I'm not.

Don't give up on her. Please, Nico.

I gave up on him. And look what happened."

"Who?" I asked.

"Gabe. I gave up on Gabe.

Those last days when he was spiraling out of control.

I didn't know what else to do. So I gave up.

And look what happened."

"Lucca, if you tried to help him,

why can't you try and help her?" I asked.

"She's too emotionally dependent on me as it is," he said.

"You know those flowers she draws?

She's like them in so many ways, Nico.

Bright and beautiful.

Lights up the world with her colorful way of seeing
things.

And she's fragile. Right now, really fragile.

Handle with care, you know?"

I know.

A flower girl indeed.

Ghost in my bedroom.

Ghost in my dreams.

Is there something to tell me?
Or is he making me pay?

Is he stuck in the past?
Is there comfort in this?

Can't he see what he's doing?
Making life hell on earth.

If that's the main point,
then I won't let him win.

He simply
can't
win.

As we run around the track,

a stray dog finds us.

A black Pomeranian,

groomed and healthy, but no tag.

We sit on the damp grass, petting him.

"Should we take him to the shelter?" Brooklyn asks me.

"Nah. I'll go door-to-door.

He's gotta live around here."

"But what about school?" she asks.

I shrug.

"Some things are more important.

Someone must be missing him.

Imagine if it were you."

She tilts her head and smiles.

"You *are* good at fixing things, aren't you?"

I feel my cheeks get warm.

"I don't know.

All I can do is try."

After dinner

my thoughts are here
and there
and everywhere
and I give up on math
before I even really start.

I keep thinking about that dog.
About Nico.
I don't know that
I've ever seen
such determination
to be good and kind
and helpful.

How often do you find
a combination of strength
and goodness
rolled into one?

And then,
it hits me like
a ton of comic books
alongside the head.

Tom Strong.

Nico is a real-life
Tom Strong.

When she calls me

I half expect to hear

a crying girl on the other end.

But no tears tonight.

"Did you find the dog's home?" she asks.

"Yeah, I did."

"Oh, good," she says. "I'm so glad.

"So, the pool tomorrow, right?"

"Yeah," I say. "Five thirty. Got your alarm set?"

She laughs. "Yes, my alarm is set.

I promise I'll be there."

"Okay, good. Try and get a good night's sleep."

"Hey, Nico?"

"Yeah?"

"Do you still like to cook?"

"Yeah. Why?"

"Just curious. Maybe we can have pasta

the night before the race.

That's what runners do, right? Load up on carbs?"

"So you an expert on racing now, Brooklyn?"

"Hardly," she says. "But I'm gonna do this thing.

I want to know what it feels like

to run across a finish line.

Despite all the obstacles and setbacks,

to go out and do it. You know?"

"Yep. I know."

"Bye, Nico."

"Bye."

I wake

to something in my hand.

My notebook
with letters to Lucca.

On the front cover
in big, black ink
in ugly, scribbly handwriting
it says,
Love is the answer. Not fear.

I toss it on the floor,
thankful he didn't give me something
dead this time.

When we meet at the pool,

she asks me for details on getting the dog home.

It was an hour and a half of knocking on doors.

I was starting to worry I'd been wrong

when a car pulled up beside me with an old guy and his wife.

They jumped out yelling, "There you are!"

Brooklyn leans against the door

leading to the women's locker room and smiles.

"I love happy endings.

So what was his name?"

"Lucky," I tell her.

"His name was Lucky."

She winks at me before she pushes on the door.

"Lucky indeed."

While I change

into my suit,
I think about that little dog, Lucky.

I was ready to give up right away.
Take him to the shelter.
Let someone else deal with him.

Not Nico.
He's not the kind of guy
to back down.

He holds on tight
when he cares strongly
about something.
Or someone.

I know Lucca
loved that about him.

I can see why.

I'm a guy.

I tell myself this every time I see Brooklyn

in her black two-piece bathing suit,

with her long legs and sweet-looking body.

I'm a guy.

It's normal to stare at an attractive girl.

Especially when she's wearing a bathing suit.

I can't help it.

I'm a guy.

Not just a guy,

but one who has pretty much been a loner

this past year and hasn't asked a girl out in so long,

I'd probably have to do something lame

like use e-mail to do the asking.

I'm such a guy.

Kyra's waiting for me

at our locker with a smile as wide
as the Golden Gate Bridge.
She grabs my hand
swings it side to side
and tells me Tyler asked her to go
to the movies with him tomorrow night.

I hug her.
"I'm happy for you.
You're going to have so much fun."

"What about you?" she asks me.

"What about me?" I say.

"You need to have some fun."

I shake my head.
"Don't worry about me.
Besides, we're going to the dance tonight, right?
That'll be fun."

"Brooklyn, what about—?"

"Stop it," I say, pointing my finger at her.
"Don't worry about me."

Brooklyn sees me

in line, paying for my everyday lunch.

"Come sit with me," she says.

"You can share my leftover pizza."

I sort of glance around, to make sure she's talking to me.

She continues. "I realize your family makes your own,

and you've probably never tasted pizza from a cardboard box.

But trust me, it's better than that crap."

She points to the processed food in my hand.

"Besides, you're training for a race. How can you eat like that?"

I rip open the bag of chips, take one out,

and put it in my mouth.

"See?" I say. "That's all there is to it."

She smiles. "Smart-ass."

I wave a chip in front of her nose.

"You know you want it."

She bites the chip out of my hand.

"Fine. We'll have chips and pizza. How's that?"

Best lunch I've had in a long time.

Friday night

bodies
bump it
grind it
shift it
crank it
work it
make it
to the
hot
loud
mad
music
on the
dance
floor.

A group of girls
pulls me up,
draws me in,
wraps me up
in their sisterly
love.

I let it
out
let it
loose
let it
go
and
I

d   n   e
            a   c

My friend Charlie

talks me into going to the game and the dance

even though I feel like going home

and doing a Rip van Winkle instead.

The game is a slaughter, our team the bloodied ones.

I think about calling it a night,

but Charlie spreads guilt on

the way he likes his cream cheese on bagels.

Thick.

So we head to the dance.

I run into Gabe's sister waiting to get in.

"Hey, Nico," she says.

"Hi, Audrey," I reply. "How's it going?"

She shrugs. "Okay."

I feel like I should say more, but what?

Besides, it's not exactly the easiest place

to have a heart-to-heart.

When we get inside, it's hot and loud,

and I feel like a popcorn kernel

being tossed into a pan of fiery hot oil.

Charlie and I take a seat in the corner,

trying to stay out of the heat.

A group of girls pull another girl up

and into the pan of popping people.

I look closer, and realize it's Brooklyn.

When I see her dancing,

having fun, it makes me smile.

It makes me glad I came.

It's fun until they play

the song *You and Me*,
and that's when I decide
to head home.

Kyra and a couple of others
beg, beg, beg
me to stay
but I
hug, hug, hug
each of them
and wave, wave, wave
and walk out
into the cool night air.

I pass by
a girl and a boy
against the wall,
hooking up,
their bodies
crocheted together
in a double love knot.

Lucky in love,
that's them.

When I see her leave,

I tell Charlie I'm going outside

to get some air.

"Brooklyn!" I yell once I'm out there.

She stops in the middle of the parking lot

 and waits for me to catch up.

"Hey, Nico."

"What's up?" I ask.

"Going home."

I grab her arm.

"Everything okay?"

She smiles.

"Yeah, I actually had fun. Until . . ."

She doesn't have to say.

I know. You can be fine, and then,

out of nowhere,

a memory blindsides you.

Distraction works for me. So I say,

"Man, can you believe they played that disco crap?"

She laughs, sticks her hip out, and puts her finger in the air.

"See you tomorrow?" I ask.

"At my place with your bike, right?"

She looks at the sky. "I wonder if it'll rain.

Wow, Nico, look at that moon."

I look up and see it shimmering behind some clouds.

She says good-bye and turns to leave,

while I stand there awhile longer,

watching the clouds and the moon

dance together.

I get home

and grab my notebook.
I open it and suddenly realize
my everyday letters
are no longer being written
every day.

That's not like me.

Not like me at all.

#289

Dear Lucca,

I miss you.
I miss your beautiful blue eyes and the love I saw in them for me.
I miss your hand that held mine.
I miss your arms around me.
I miss your lips on mine.
I miss your laughter.
I miss the way you called me Brooker the Looker
I miss your voice and the sweet everythings you whispered in my ear.
I miss the drawings you showed me before anyone else.
I miss our midnight conversations for no other reason than to say, "I love you."
I miss how I felt safe when I was with you.
I miss you, Lucca.
For my whole life, I will miss you.

Love always,
Brooklyn

Ma's awake

when I get home.

Just sitting at the kitchen table,

her hands glued to a coffee mug

that's as empty as a rain barrel

on a hot August day.

"You all right, Ma?"

Her sigh says she's not

while her words say, "I suppose."

She does this.

Every now and then, she sinks into a pit of despair

and Pop and I wonder if this is it.

If this is the one time we can't pull her out,

if she'll just sink deeper and deeper

until she's so far gone,

there's no way to reach her.

I stand behind her and start rubbing her neck and shoulders.

"You should go to bed," I tell her. "It's late."

"I suppose," she says again. "Did you have fun?"

And because it's good for Ma to hear

and maybe me, too, I say,

"Yeah. I think I did."

This time

my dream
begins in the cemetery
where I'm visiting Lucca's grave,
my arms weighed down
by dozens of beautiful roses,
their sweet fragrance
surrounding me.

I'm fascinated by the color
of those roses.
A deep,
rich,
luscious
red.

Everything else
is gray.

The sky.
The tombstones.
The ground.
The trees.

I bend down to put the
red roses
on his grave,
when he appears.

Gabe.

My arms extend
as if I'm a bird
ready to take flight,
and a flurry of

red   red   red
    red   red   red
red   red   red

drops silently
to the ground.

Then I turn
and run,
wishing I really could fly
into the grayness
above the red,
away from the fear.

Away from him.

When I sit up,
forcing myself awake,
I'm thankful for the lit lamp
on my nightstand
that lately, I never turn off.

And then I see it.

A deep,
rich,
luscious
red
rose
laying at the foot
of my bed.

It's not the best day

for a bike ride.

I get up,

an hour before we're supposed to meet.

Rain pounds the roof,

like Mother Nature is throwing one hell of a tantrum.

I call Brooklyn and suggest we swim again instead.

I can tell she's upset.

Something's happened.

There's a hint of something in her voice.

Sadness?

Fear?

What?

She won't say.

And she doesn't want to swim.

"Well, we have to do something," I tell her.

"Let's have a picnic," she says.

Not exactly what I had in mind.

"Come over," she continues.

"My dad isn't here. He's doing emergency surgery.

We'll have a picnic in my living room."

Maybe this is it.

Maybe she's finally going to tell me.

I want to tell him.

I want him to come over here
and I will tell him
about these nightmares
and the rose in my room
and how Gabe is chasing me,
and watching me
and giving me things
in the dead of the night.

I want to tell him.

But I don't know if I can.

I want her to tell me

what's going on.

How can I get her to do that?

What would Lucca have done?

He would have told her to draw

and then looked for clues there.

That's what artists do, right?

They express themselves through their art.

I need to get her drawing.

Only problem is,

she draws flowers,

and there aren't a whole lot of flowers

blooming in January.

Unless . . .

While I wait for Nico to arrive,

I peel and slice apples
because a pie is good and wholesome
and I'm feeling the need
for some of that right about now.

Green skins lay in the sink,
shredded like raincoats
after the storm has passed.

When the pie dish is full,
I spread a blanket of pastry
across the naked pieces
of golden fruit.

I tuck them in,
my fingers carefully crimping the dough
in just the right places.

Forty minutes later,
the smell of apples mixed with
cinnamon and sugar
greets Nico at the door.

He smiles and pulls a dozen red roses
from behind his back.

Hands to my mouth,
I jump back as if he's just tried to hand me
a dozen grenades.

What the *hell* is going on?

This isn't good.

The look on her face.

Does she hate roses?

Are they too commercial or something?

"I thought maybe you'd want to draw," I say.

"But you don't like roses?"

"No, it's just . . ."

I step inside.

"Don't stop," I plead. "Tell me. What is it?"

She reaches out and takes them.

"They're gorgeous. Thank you."

The timer lets out an annoying buzz.

She practically throws the roses

on the counter as she runs to the stove

to get a pie that looks like

it just stepped out of a magazine.

"You baked that?

Wow. Is there anything you can't do?"

She starts to speak.

Then stops.

Why the *hell* won't she talk to me?

When he asks me

if there's anything I can't do,
I start to say,
Yes, I can't stop Gabe from haunting me.

But I glance at the flowers
and wonder if there's more going on
than I understand.

As the sky opens up
and pounds the roof
in a rage of raindrops,
we spread a tablecloth
across the living room floor
and feast on pita bread with hummus,
crunchy carrots and juicy grapes,
cups of warm tomato soup with basil,
and apple pie, of course.

He's very sweet,
talking to fill the empty gaps
giving me tips about the race.

I look at him and wonder.
Wonder about things.
There's so much we haven't talked about.

"Do you ever dream about Lucca?" I ask.
"Sorry. Another random question, I know."

He nods.
"Do you?"

"Hardly ever.
Even though I wish for that every night."

"Sometimes it can be a downer though.
You know, like I wake up, and reality hits me."

I nod.

And before I can stop myself, I ask,
"Do you ever dream about Gabe?"

He shakes his head, no.

"Do you?" he asks.

"Once or twice," I say quickly.
"I was just curious.
You haven't really talked about him.
About what happened."

"He was an idiot, that's what happened," he says.
"There are a hundred places to go if you're having trouble.
If you need help and don't know what to do."

As he gets up and takes stuff to the counter,
I think about that.

And what I think is that
when you're completely alone
and deep inside yourself
with feelings no one else can understand,
there really aren't a hundred places to go.

It's like if I woke up one day
and looked outside and saw purple trees
and red grass and green dogs,
is there anyone I could tell who would understand?

No.
There'd be no one.
It's exactly like that.

He saw purple trees
and red grass and green dogs
while no one else did.

And maybe,
he just got tired
of seeing them.

I decide we need

to lighten the mood,

so I ask her to show me some of her art.

She doesn't say a word.

Just looks at me with eyes of uncertainty.

"You really want to see?"

"Yes," I say. "I really do."

She leaves and returns with a big black book,

and we sit together on the love seat,

the book laid in her lap

as tenderly as if it were an infant.

On the first page, on the left side, is a photo of a sunflower,

and on the right, her artistic version.

The colors and the lighting,

so right on,

all I can say,

in a whisper of wonderment,

is "Wow."

Page after page of

blues and purples, oranges and yellows,

mums and lilacs, daisies and daffodils.

The last one is a single rose,

on top of a casket.

My brother's casket.

So much for lightening the mood.

I haven't drawn

in so long.

Since he died.

Looking at these pictures,
I wonder,
did that part of me
that flourished around him,
like prized perennials
under a tender gardener's care,
die along with him?

Or am I just dormant,
able to bloom again someday
when love finally decides
to shine on me
again?

When her dad comes home,

she introduces me as her friend.

She doesn't tell him I'm Lucca's brother.

Would he think that's weird,

us hanging out together?

Is it weird?

Do I care?

After Nico leaves

Dad drills me.

I tell him he's just a friend
I know from school
who's helping me train for a race.

Then he wants to know what kind of race
and why I'm doing *that*
and do I like this guy and is that why I'm doing it
and blah blah blah.

I guess it's good he's interested
because most of the time
it seems like he cares more about ESPN
than me.

After I've told him
what he wants to know,
he says, "And look, he brought you roses.
What a coincidence.
You saw the rose I left you this morning, right?"

"You left the rose?"

"Someone sent us flowers at the office.
To say thanks.
I let one of the admins take them home.
But I brought one home for you.
And then I forgot to give it to you last night."

My dad left me a rose.
Not a ghost.

Thank God.
Not a ghost.

This morning I found

A Cry for Help
in my gym bag.
He's still worried.
And I wish I knew
what to do about that.

This morning I found

a few of the letters to Lucca
torn up and tossed around,
like confetti.

Why?

My words,
my heart,
my soul,
shredded by someone
who seems intent
on hurting me.

Why?

Tears slide down my face
as I pick my heart
off the floor.

Fear controls you.
Stop the fear.
Love is the answer. Not fear.

Does Gabe want me to love him?
How can I love him
when right now,
I hate him more
than I've ever hated anyone
in my whole life?

I sob into a fistful
of shredded words.

Because words matter.
And so do I.

When we meet up

at the pool,

she's cold and distant.

It's like one step forward,

two steps back with her.

Just when it feels like

we're making progress,

something happens

and we're running backward.

I don't know what else to do.

What else can I do?

The water

feels extra cold today,
matching the temperature
of my heart.

I swim,
hoping the water
might smooth things out
once again and
wash my troubles away.

But nothing is smooth today.
It's choppy and hard
and I tire easily.
When I finally can't take
the failure anymore,
I get out.

Nico's in a swimming trance.
Doesn't even notice me.
I slip out quietly,
away from the cold, harsh water
into the cold, harsh world.

When I realize she's gone,

I start to go after her.

But I change my mind.

Because obviously, she doesn't

want to include me in whatever's going on.

Whatever's bringing her so much pain.

She starts to give, then pulls back,

gives, then pulls back.

I hate tug-of-war.

It seems so pointless.

And I'm not sure I can pull any harder.

All I can do is keep showing up.

Keep engaging her in life.

Keep trying.

I'm standing

at a crossroads
in the middle of nowhere.

One path leads into
thick, black trees
with weird noises.
It's dark.
Creepy.

The other path
leads into the sun,
with colorful wildflowers
growing on both sides.
Birds are chirping,
and farther down the path,
a large oak tree
with plenty of shade awaits.

I have to choose one.
Any second, I'll hear
his footsteps behind me,
and I'll have to choose.

The choice seems obvious.
But something tells me
it's a trick.
The sunny path that looks safe
can't be as it seems.

Nothing is ever as it seems.

So I begin running,
through the dark forest,
branches reaching out
and grabbing me as I do.

I hear him coming.
Closer and closer.

He grabs me and yells,
"Why do you keep choosing fear?"

I wake up screaming.

Daddy comes running.
Flips the light and
sits on my bed.

I crawl out,
squeeze next to him,
and let him wrap me up
in his arms.

And we stay that way
for a long time.

I swear

I left my keys where I always do.

The kitchen table, by the napkin holder.

But this morning, they're not there.

I look everywhere—

jacket, pants, dresser, bathroom, ignition.

Nothing.

Finally, twenty minutes later and ridiculously

late for school, I go back to the kitchen table.

And there they are.

Gone before.

Now here.

Apparently just like my brother.

Who always did enjoy making me sweat the small stuff.

As I walk out the door, I laugh.

I miss you, Lucca.

Man, I miss you.

Nico's all happy

and cheerful as we run,
telling me a story about a guy at school
who made a fool of himself
in front his dream girl.
Apparently, the guy didn't know
she was watching.

God, Nico is just too happy.
He doesn't have a freaking care
in the world.

Well, of course he doesn't.
His world is all about
running and biking,
puppy dogs and potato chips.

When he laughs at himself
for the third time,
I stop and yell,
"Shut the hell up, Nico.
It's not funny, okay?
God. You think everything is funny?
Well, let me tell you.
It's not."

He stares at me like I just threw
rocks at his head.

And then I turn around
and go home.

Our paths don't cross

at school, so later, I call her up.

"I don't think everything is funny," I tell her.

"I'm sorry, Nico. It's not you. It's me."

"It's all right," I say. "Some mornings are like that.

I have an idea, though. A different kind of workout.

Can you be ready in thirty minutes?"

"What? Um, yeah, I guess."

"Great."

"Wait, what should I wear?"

I almost quip back with something inappropriate,

but I stop myself.

"Jeans. T-shirt. Tennis shoes."

Silence.

"See you in a few!"

Did I really just do that?

Pirate's Bay Miniature Golf

greets us with neon lights
and eighteen holes of fun and adventure
in a big warehouse.

We hit the balls
through old ships,
around treasure chests,
and up and over bridges.

Four hits,
five hits,
six.

Hole after hole.

Ten smiles,
Eleven smiles,
twelve.

Hole after hole.

No ghosts,
no ghosts,
none.

Hole after glorious hole.

Around hole 7

I'm all stressed about my score,

about trying to get the elusive hole-in-one.

She teases me, asks if my lifelong dream

is to be king of the putt-putt.

Before I know what she's doing,

she grabs my score sheet,

rips it into little pieces,

and throws it in the sky,

a shower of confetti raining down on us.

"Now let's have some fun," she says.

And that's just what we do.

On the last hole,

I get a hole-in-one
which sends me into
a squealing fit of joy,
like a little kid at the first sight
of the tree Christmas morning.

Nico looks at me,
looks at the hole,
takes a deep breath,
and hits his ball.

Like magic,
that neon green ball
goes right for the hole
and drops in with a
resounding plunk.

I give him a high five.
"Well done, King," I tell him.

He smiles.
"Actually, hate to burst your bubble
but I think it's rigged."

"You mean everyone gets a hole-in-one?" I ask.

They want people to leave
happy.

And I'm pretty sure
we do.

On the way home,

we're quiet.

A song by The Fray comes on—

How to Save a Life.

"I love this song," she says as she turns it up.

The haunting music and words

speak about trying to help someone.

And I know what she's thinking.

I just hope she'll open up and talk about it.

When we pull up to her house,

 she turns and says, "I didn't do enough."

"I didn't do enough to help him."

"No," I say. "Don't play that game, Brooklyn.

What happened to Gabe has nothing to do with you.

You were hurting too, and you did the best you could.

We all did."

She nods, and tears well up in her eyes.

Here we are, the weather changing again.

"Brooklyn," I say softly, "listen to me.

If this is what you're struggling with, let it go."

"I'm trying," she whispers.

I reach up and wipe the single tear

that manages to escape.

"You can do this," I tell her.

"You are so strong, Brooklyn.

Stronger than you know. Believe in that, okay?"

When he tells me

how strong I am,
something flares up inside of me.
It makes me want to be strong
even if I don't feel that way
most of the time.

I feel a shift.
A shift in my heart.

I don't know exactly
what it is
or what it means
but I definitely feel it.

There's something about Nico
that makes me want
to be a better person.

And so I tell myself,
I will be.

As I'm getting ready

to head out to the track,

I find a note from Pop

with a guy's phone number.

Hey, Nico—

Give Rob a call.

He might have a job for you.

Bagging groceries.

As I go to stick the note in my pocket,

I notice writing on the other side.

It says *Hey, Lucca—*

And then it's crossed out.

He started writing to him instead of me.

He's still wanting him back.

And wanting me out of here.

We meet up

at the track where he tells me
he really needs to run
at his own pace today.

I tell him to go ahead
and I watch as he becomes
a man possessed.

He laps me two,
three,
four times,
never slowing down.

After an hour,
I've done all I can do,
but the look on his face
tells me he doesn't want to stop.

So, I quietly walk across the track,
and leave the gift I brought him
in his truck.

It's a gift bag
with a plastic snake inside,
along with a note:

Dear Nico,

Please don't be afraid—you ARE helping me.
As for snakes? You should be very afraid.

Love,
Brooklyn

When I see

the gift bag sitting on the seat of my truck,

something inside of me snaps.

A gift means something.

I open it and yeah, it's silly and nothing special,

but even a silly little gift means something.

This is heading to a place it can't go.

I'm not him.

I pound my hand on the steering wheel.

I'M NOT HIM!

Everyone wants him.

Not me.

Yesterday and today

Nico didn't show.
Yesterday, I swam without him.
Today, I ran without him.

I start to call him
to make sure he's okay,
but I freeze up.

It's not like he's sick,
because I saw him at school.

So what's he going to say?

That he got tired of my moods
changing faster than he can run?

That he got tired of trying
to lift me up all the time?

That he simply got tired
of me?

So I leave him alone,
because that's obviously
what he wants.

But I still run.
I still swim.
Harder than I ever have before.
Because I want to do this thing.
Show him I am strong.
And that he really has helped me,
more than he'll ever know.

I've messed up.

It's like I was trying to make

something easy like pasta carbonara

and in trying to make it the best

pasta carbonara ever,

throwing this and that into it,

I've ruined it.

I feel like I've totally ruined this thing

with Brooklyn.

I don't even know what's happened,

but something's changed.

It just feels different.

Leaving a gift for me,

that's not workout partners.

That's *different*.

I run into Gabe's sister,

Audrey, in the bathroom at school.

We wash our hands, side by side,
and I glance at her reflection
in the mirror.

She looks okay.
Normal.
Good, even.
Clear, blue eyes.
Nice color to her cheeks.
She smiles at me.
I smile back.

Just two girls in the bathroom,
doing what girls do.

I should say something.
But what?
And what good would it do anyway?

She leaves,
and I stand there,
studying myself in the mirror.

I look okay.
Good even.

My reflection tells one story.
My heart, a different one.

The difference is,
hearts don't lie.
Mirrors do.

As I run,

I find myself

running toward the cemetery.

I start to resist and then decide

to go with it.

The early morning fog seems to

swallow me as I run,

allowing me to see only

a few feet in front of me.

Arriving at the cemetery gate,

the morning light yet to appear,

all the elements of death

are here.

Darkness.

Solitude.

Pain.

All of it surrounds me and

I'm surprised when I realize

how familiar it feels.

I turn and run the other way.

Whatever it is I want or need,

it's not that.

When I wake up,

I sense that
something's not right.

I look around.
The light is still on.
The windows are still closed.
The room is still neat.

It's just as I left it.

But as I get up,
get dressed to go run,
the feeling doesn't leave me

Something's not right.

As I go to my door,
it's then that I see it.
My stomach tightens
and my legs shake.
On the full-length mirror
on the back of my door,
is a note torn from my notebook
and stuck to the mirror.
Across the words I'd written to Lucca,
in big, black letters,
it says:

WHY DO YOU RUN?
WHY ARE YOU AFRAID?

After dinner,

I go to Lucca's room
and shut the door.
I look around and think
about the bed he hated to make,
the clothes he hated to put away,
and the dishes he hated to wash.
He was a slob.
I can't stand a mess.
I want things neat.
I'd never let my room get this messy.
Ma used to bug him about it
all the time.
Not once has she ever had to tell me
to clean my room.
It's a little thing, I guess.
But it's something.

I dream of a room

crisp and white.

I'm at a party,
in a doll-like house
filled with porcelain-like people,
painted to perfection,
their smiles and laughter
buzzing like bees,
stinging my ears
because this is not at all
funny.

I see him
from across the room.

He looks at me,
and walks toward me.
Frowning.

He stands out among
the delightful dolls,
his grayish face
sunken and hollow.

But no one notices.

He just walks,
his eyes holding mine
across the crowded room.

If I turn and run,
where will I go?

If I stand and stay,
what do I do?

Closer
and closer
he comes.

The dolls keep
chattering away,
and laughing,
louder and louder.

"What's so funny?" I scream.

Silence.
Stares.
Sadness.

My sadness
among their smiles
frozen in place.

Out of the corner
of my eye,
I see Nico,
one of the dolls.

"Help me," I cry out.
"Please.
Help me!"

"No," he yells.
"Help yourself!"

I sit up,
panting and sweating,
alone in my room,
the clock glowing 4:56 a.m.

I search my room,
looking for my notebook
needing to write in it.

Where is it?
When did I write in it last?
I stop and realize,
not for quite a while.

And I realize,
not once,
until now,
have I missed it.

Pop's at the table

drinking coffee, reading the paper.

I sit down next to him with a bagel.

"Did you call about the job?" he asks.

"No," I say. "Been too busy."

He sets the paper down.

"Pop, I'll get a job this summer, okay?

I'm training now. For a race in April.

It's important to me.

I need you to understand, this is important to me."

He's quiet, his brown eyes thougtful.

"I didn't realize," he says. "You never told me.

What race is this?"

So while I eat my bagel

and he drinks his coffee,

I tell him.

And when I'm done telling him,

he says, "Well, Nico, that's quite the endeavor.

I find it honorable that you want to finish what you've

   started.

I wish you good luck, son."

He pats my arm before he picks up his paper.

I look at him and realize,

maybe I overreacted.

Maybe more than once.

Mom calls me,

giving the notebook search party
a much-needed break.

When she asks what I'm up to lately,
I tell her about the training,
which prompts lots of questions.

When we're done,
I hand the phone to Daddy
so he can talk to the boys.

Over and over again,
he tells them he misses them.
He loves them.
Like he's afraid
he'll never talk to them again.

The truth is,
we both understand,
you just never know.

I think back

to last Saturday

and how she shared

pie, pictures, and pieces of her heart.

Today, I get a seven-mile bike ride

alone.

Pretty pathetic.

Unless . . .

Back in my room,

I tear everything apart
looking for the notebook.

It's gone.
Vanished.
Taken by a ghost, I assume.

Damn him.
Damn him for coming in here
and messing with my life.
Damn him for giving me
cryptic messages
that make no sense.

I have to figure it out.
I have to figure out
what it all means.
And I have to figure out
what to do to get him
to leave me alone.

I used to work out

by myself all the time.
But this morning,
when I thought about not seeing her again,
it felt about as wrong
as going to school on a Saturday.
Her dad answers the door,
and invites me in.
I wait while he goes and gets her.
When she finally comes down the stairs
in polka-dot pajamas,
her hair sticking out on one side of her head
and smooshed flat on the other,
I fight the urge
to go over and hug her.
Because she *is* more
than a workout partner.
She's become my friend.

"Nico.

What are you doing here?"

"Thought we'd go for a ride."

"I, uh, I didn't expect you.
I mean, after last week."

"Yeah, sorry about that.
Had some stuff going on."

"You could have called.
E-mailed. Something."

"I know. I'm sorry.
Forgive me?"

I start to pace the floor.
"I'm not sure I can go right now.
I've got some stuff going on myself."

"Can I help?" he asks.

I want to say—

Help?
You want to help?
Get rid of him!
Just make him go away
and leave me alone!

But I don't.

Instead I start to shake.
My whole body starts to shake
and I have to sit down.

Once on the sofa,
I put my head in my hands
and tell myself not to cry.
He doesn't need to see me cry
again.

I take a deep breath.
Then I look at him.

"No, Nico, you can't help.
I wish you could.
But you can't."

I sit down

at the other end of the sofa,

silence sitting on the cushion

between us.

Finally, I have to try.

Tell me," I whisper to her.

"Brooklyn, please.

Just *tell* me.

What's really going on?

You can trust me."

I think about that.

Trust me.

Have faith in me.

And yet, why should she?

There's nothing to prove she can trust me

except my words.

She trusted him.

She had faith in him.

And he left her forever.

Something tells me she's not forgetting that

anytime soon.

He's giving me

an open door.

Do I go?
Do I walk through?
What's on the other side?
Once I go through,
I can't go back.

Once through, I'm there.
My nightmares become his.
My fears not my own.

Will it change anything?
Will it change how he sees me?
Will it change us?

He reaches over,
takes my hand,
and with his thumb,
gently caresses it,
trying to tell me
it will be okay.

I jerk my hand away
and stand up.

I slam the door
closed.

We go from zero to sixty

in about a second:
From sitting there,
going nowhere,
trying to get her to say something
to getting up,
her saying, "Let's go,
I'll change my clothes,
then we'll hit the road."
Just like that we're moving
and yet really
we're right back
where we started.

We ride around town

for an hour
and then he stops at a park
a few blocks from his house.

He doesn't say anything.
He just goes to the swing,
sits down, and starts pumping.
I take a seat next to him.

We don't talk.
We just swing.

There is comfort
in the act of swinging.

True,
unexpected
comfort.

"You want to jump?" he asks.
"See who can go the farthest?"

I shake my head.

"I just want to swing," I say.

And so we do.

Swinging is safe.

There's nothing to fear, unlike jumping.

Taking that leap requires courage.

So we quietly swing, like she wants.

I understand wanting that.

Needing that.

When she's had enough, she slows down

and simply steps off.

As we walk back to our bikes

she stops and stands there,

looking up at the sky,

big, puffy clouds floating by.

"It feels like I've lost so much," she says softly.

"What have I got left?"

I grab her arm and pull, just enough to get her walking.

"Me, Brooklyn.

You've got me."

As we walk,

I tell him, "My mom loves clouds.

When I was little,
we'd lay in the backyard,
watching the clouds float by.

We'd shout out the shapes we saw.
A cat,
a tree,
a dinosaur.

One time I said,
'I see the sun!'

She reached over and covered my eyes.
'Don't look at the sun, Brooklyn.
It can blind you!'

I didn't mean the real sun.
I meant a sun made of clouds.

When I explained it to her,
we laughed until we cried."

We stand at our bikes
and he smiles.
"Isn't it funny," he says,
"how easily things can be misunderstood?"

I nod.

"You know that plastic snake you gave me?
It kind of freaked me out."

I laugh. "It did?"

"Not like that.
I mean, the note and the gift bag.
I didn't know—"

"What?" I say.

But then, I get it.
He thought it meant something.
Something more.

"Oh. Oh! Well, I mean, it was just,
you know, a funny gift.
To say thank you.
Really. That's all."

He starts getting on his bike.
"I know. It was sweet."

And as we ride off,
I try to figure out if he meant
it freaked him out in a good way
or freaked him out in a bad way.

That's pretty much
what I think about
all the way home.

It was just a funny gift.

A funny gift?

Well, what did I want her to say?

I don't know.

Wait.

Maybe I do.

Oh, no.

Do I?

And if I wanted her to say that,

well, that means the unthinkable.

And the unthinkable is pretty much

a totally impossible situation.

Isn't it?

Confusion

fills me up.

Like thick, ugly goo,
it fills my head,
my heart,
my stomach,
until I feel sick.

Do I feel that way?

Did I want the silly gift
to mean something more?

Am I disappointed that
it might have done the opposite
of what I wanted it to do?

Yes.
Yes.

Oh my God.

Yes.

We're running

this morning,

through the neighborhood

so she doesn't get too used to track running,

which is different from street running.

"Isn't running all the same?" she asks.

"That's like me asking you if art is all the same.

Which it's not, right?"

She nods.

"Some people draw flowers," I continue.

"And some people draw cartoons," she says.

And then it's my turn to simply nod.

Lucca brought us together.

So why do I feel annoyed

when it feels like he's right here

in between us?

I think bringing up

Lucca's art made Nico
feel uncomfortable,
like wearing a wool sweater
without a shirt underneath.

So I change the subject
and ask him about "the zone."

I've always wondered
what runners mean
when they say they hit "the zone."

He tells me
it's this place you find
when you're running
where everything feels right.

Where your breathing,
your stride,
your temperature,
everything feels good,
maybe even better than good,
and when you get there,
to this place,
you feel like you could go forever.

"Is that why runners keep running?" I ask.

"Pretty much," he says.
"You wait, Brooklyn.
One of these days you'll find it.
And then you'll be hooked."

As I stop to walk
to catch my breath,
it's hard to imagine
ever finding the zone.

But then,
a year ago,
it was hard to imagine
ever getting out of bed.

And now look at me.

After we run,

I talk her into breakfast.

It's Sunday, so we have time.

We go to Pop's favorite place,

 The Whistle Stop Café near the train station.

She orders coffee, eggs and toast.

I order pancakes with a side of hash browns.

All around us,

black and white photos of trains

and people going places.

She asks where I'd go

if I could hop a train and ride somewhere.

I say Washington, D.C.

for the monuments and museums.

She says Maine

for faraway fun in the snow.

I tell her I thought she might say Vegas

to see her mom and brothers.

"You miss them?" I ask.

A simple question.

She nods.

Sips her coffee.

Looks out the window.

Then she turns and starts talking

and for the next fifteen minutes,

pausing only when our food comes,

she gives me anything but

a simple answer.

As we leave,

I start to say,
thanks for the nice time.
Thanks for being easy
to talk to.
Thanks for working out with me
and giving me the
confidence I need.

I start to say a lot of things.

But in the end,
all I say is,
"See you tomorrow."

I'm listening

to the new Killers CD

doing homework

when *Goodnight, Travel Well*

comes on.

Dark.

Eerie.

Sad.

The room gets cold.

The light on my desk flickers.

He's here.

He loved The Killers.

I sit there, knowing he's listening too.

I close my eyes,

remembering,

wanting it to be different,

hating the world cause it's not.

When the last note fades,

the room warms up,

and the light brightens.

He's gone.

Goodnight, Lucca.

Travel well.

It's late

and I can't fall asleep.
I go downstairs
to get a snack,
where I find Daddy
in his bathrobe,
his head in his hands
at the kitchen table.

When I ask what's wrong
all he can say is,
"I miss them."

He stands up,
hugs me,
and lets out a sob.

Clearly I'm not the only one
in the house
battling demons.

I'm sound asleep

when I hear a ring.

I pick my pants off the floor

and pull out my phone.

1:09 a.m.

Brooklyn says she can't sleep.

Her dad misses her brothers.

She misses them too.

Silence.

I rub my eyes trying to get

what she's saying and why she's saying it

at one o'clock in the morning.

"Sing me a lullaby," she says.

I laugh.

"Please, Nico. I think it will help."

"Help what?" I ask. "To upset you even more?"

Silence.

"You could never upset me," she says softly.

"Please?"

So I take a deep breath,

and start to sing,

making it up as I go along,

to the tune of *Twinkle Twinkle Little Star*.

"In the quiet of the night,

Brooklyn baby tucked in tight.

Close your eyes, everything's all right.

Dreams will take you to the light.

Like a star, you're lovely and bright.

So sleep baby girl, sleep all night."

I thought she'd laugh,

tell me I'm horrible,

and a singer is the last thing I should be.

Instead she says, "That is the best song ever."

"Yeah, right."

"Thanks, Nico," she says. "I think I can sleep now."

"Sweet dreams, Brooklyn."

"From your lips to God's ears, Nico."

After we hang up,

I lie there for hours

hoping at least one of us

is sleeping.

When I wake up

I whisper prayers of thanks.

Thank you for a night free of ghosts and nightmares.
Thank you for another day of living.
Thank you for a race that gives me purpose.
Thank you for a lullaby last night.
Thank you for the boy who sang it.

I think he called me lovely in the song.
Did he?
Yeah, he did.
And I feel my heart
do a dance of joy
at the thought.

While we run

this morning,

I talk to her about the race,

and how transitions can be hard.

Getting out of the water,

getting ready for the bike.

Getting off the bike,

getting ready for the run.

I tell her, keep your transitions simple.

Don't sweat them too much.

Most mistakes in transition happen

because people are in too much of a hurry

and do stupid stuff.

I tell her that eventually

we'll need to practice transitions.

We'll need to swim and then bike.

We'll need to bike and then run.

She looks at me.

"I can do this, right?"

I smile and grab her arm.

"Absolutely."

"You're always so confident," she says.

If only she knew the truth . . .

Kyra's sitting with Tyler

at lunch, smiling and laughing.
I sit at a table with some other girls,
leaving the lovebirds alone because
that's what they want,
even if she'd never tell me that.

As I eat,
I notice Audrey in line.
Another girl comes up to her,
talks to her,
and Audrey pretends to listen
but by the look on her face,
you can tell she's a million miles away.

How many days was I like that?
Pretending to listen, but not hearing a word?
Pretending to care when I hated it all?
Pretending to live when I was dying inside?

Too many to count,
that's how many.

I'm packing up my books

for homework when I see something

in the corner of my locker.

Something that wasn't there Friday.

I pull out *A Cry for Help*.

And just as I do, Brooklyn walks up.

"Are we swimming or riding tomorrow?" she asks.

She sees the book.

"What's that? You reading it for Language Arts or something?"

She takes it out of my hand.

Opens it.

Has he written anything in it?

Torn any of the pages in a weird, ghostly way?

I take it back before she has a chance to see if he has.

"Nah. Someone loaned it to me. Thought I might like it."

"What's it about?" she asks.

I shrug. "I have no idea.

So, about tomorrow."

She walks out with me,

the whole time I'm thinking,

what else can I do, Lucca?

What else am I supposed to do?

The worst night yet.

Another nightmare
in a graveyard,
being chased
past the headstones
only to wake up
to find the light I'd left on
now turned off.

With the awful smell in the room,
of dirt and death
combined with a coldness in the air,
I wondered if I was Jonah,
swallowed whole by a whale.

I reached for the lamp,
but before I switched it on,
I saw him there,
floating in the corner,
ever-so-slightly glowing,
a dark red aura around him.

I sat there, frozen,
until he let out a moan of words
so deep,
so frightening,
so dark,
it made me run from my room,
down to the kitchen,
where I turned on all the lights
and started grabbing pans
from the cupboard,
thinking I'd make hot cocoa,
but secretly hoping the loud noise
would scare ghostly Gabe away.

Now, my shaky hands
grab the milk from the fridge
as I remember his words.

You can't run forever.

She calls me

as I'm on my way to the pool.

Her quivery voice makes me wonder

if we'll be going today.

She asks me to come to her house,

so I quickly change directions.

When I get there, she's standing outside

in jeans and a hoody,

her arms wrapped around herself,

trying to stay warm.

When she climbs in,

I notice her red cheeks and chapped lips.

"Man, Brooklyn, how long you been outside?"

Her teeth start chattering. "A long time."

I blast the heat

and take her hands in mine and rub them.

She looks at me, her eyes filled with fear.

"Shit, what is it?" I ask.

She doesn't speak.

Not a word.

Instead, she slowly leans in

and kisses me.

What am I doing?

I'm kissing Nico.
God, I'm kissing him.
His lips are so
warm
and soft
and he tastes like
mint toothpaste
and I want more
so I open my mouth
and softly put my tongue there
waiting for his to meet mine,
and when it does,
heat replaces cold
and I feel like I'm going to
burn up
everywhere.

His hand runs down my hair,
my shoulder,
my back
and stops there,
pressing me to him
and something about that
makes me pull away.

When I open my eyes,
I remember who I'm with.

Nico.
Just Nico.
But he's not just Nico.
He's Lucca's *brother*.

As it happens,

I feel my heart running laps in my chest.

She's simultaneously hot and cold.

Her lips,

her hair,

her skin,

her whole friggin' body

is a burning icicle.

God, I could kiss her forever.

So when she pulls away,

my heart stops in its tracks.

I can tell from her eyes

she didn't mean it.

It was a moment of weakness.

Needing someone.

Anyone.

Not me, specifically.

A warm body.

Of course, not me.

It could never be me.

Not after him.

I know she's going to say

it was a mistake.

My heart holds its breath

and waits.

"I'm sorry, Nico.

I shouldn't have done that.
I'm just so confused.
About everything."

He tucks my hair
behind my ear like he did
that first day we talked.
He's so tender.
So kind.
So good.

But this can't happen.
One Ferrari can't replace
another.

"Brooklyn, you need to know—"

"Please don't, Nico.
Remember what you said about transitions?
They can be hard.
But we have to keep them simple.
We're in transition.
Our lives are one big transition.
Getting used to being without him.
But this, you and me, it's not the answer.
If we do this, I'm afraid we're making a mistake.
Just like you said.
Keep the transitions simple."

He starts to say something,
but I don't let him.

"I'm sorry, Nico.
I can't see you anymore.
I have to figure everything out by myself.
I know that now."

And then I get out
and run back into my house,
which is pretty much
the last place I want to be,
but really the only place I have.

I want to tell her

transitions in life are different

from transitions in a race.

But she doesn't give me a chance.

As quickly as she came into my life, she's gone.

Now what am I supposed to do?

Keep running, like always?

It's worked before.

But now?

I don't know.

I tell my dad

I've got bad cramps
and he lets me stay home.

I stay in the family room,
on the couch,
in front of the TV,
with every light on.

When it's time for bed,
I don't move.
I just pretend to fall asleep
on the couch
and he lets me be.

When I fall asleep for real,
I'm a butterfly,
floating from flower to flower.
There's no color but I still feel
peaceful and happy.
At home.

A nice dream
until a shadow comes,
and swallows the warm sunshine.

Hands are after me.
Large hands.
Reaching.
Grasping.
Wanting.

My tiny wings
move quickly,
as I fly through bushes
and over the hollyhocks
and cosmos.

Faster and faster I fly,
not wanting the same fate
as the moth in my room.

And yet as I look
at Mother Nature's handiwork
all around me,
with no color, no life, no texture,
I think of the gray life
I've committed myself to,
and realize perhaps his fate
is my own after all.

I wonder if

we should try and talk about it,

about us,

but Brooklyn is nowhere to be found.

I decide to give her what she's obviously asking for.

Space.

For now, anyway.

At lunch, I think about sitting in my truck alone

with my crazy, mixed-up thoughts for company,

and decide that sounds as appealing as running in a blizzard

So I grab a sandwich and take a seat

next to Charlie and some other guys.

"Hey, Nico," he says. "What's up?

How's training going?"

"You know. Making progress."

"Progress is good," he says.

Damn it.

We were making progress.

Nightmare

after nightmare
after nightmare.
Always gray.
Disgustingly dreary
and gray.

Wake up,
sleep again,
wake up,
toss and turn,
drift to sleep,
wake up.

He's there,
around every corner.
No matter what I do,
where I go,
he's there.

I cry,
so tired of it all,
missing Nico
and the way he made me feel.

It's so right with Nico.
And yet so wrong.

Right and wrong.
Black and white.
And many shades
of gray.

I want color in my life.
Color in my dreams.

The colors of
buttercups and pansies,
poppies and chrysanthemums,
lilies and hydrangeas.

Color, beautiful color.

Lucca is haunting me

like never before.

Every night,

in different ways,

whispering,

moving,

breathing,

writing,

Brooklyn,

Brooklyn,

help her,

help Brooklyn.

Tonight,

he plays *Fix You*

over and

over and

over again

until I can't take it anymore.

I get up, take the CD out, and snap it in half.

"Don't you get it, I can't!" I yell.

A minute later, Ma and Pop come running.

"It was just a nightmare," I tell them.

Ma gives me a hug before they shuffle back to bed,

while I lie in mine

covered by feelings of worry and guilt.

Brooklyn doesn't want to see me.

She doesn't even want to talk to me.

How can I possibly help her now?

Best friends

are together
through it all,
like soil and roots,
one needing the other,
through chilling winters,
scorching summers,
through hailstorms
and lightning strikes.
They weather it
together.

So when Kyra calls,
I tell her about Nico.
How I don't want
to be thinking of him
but I am,
and why does that feel
so wrong?

Talking it through with her,
not to find a resolution
but to have someone hear me
is just what I need
to help me feel stronger,
grounded,
in this hailstorm
called life.

The hours crawl

like time has decided to slow down

and take a vacation.

I go to the pool before school,

the water especially cold this morning,

matching the temperature of my heart.

I miss her.

There's no confusion there.

As to what to do about it,

that's another story.

I managed

to convince Daddy
to let me stay home all week.

He was preoccupied,
getting stuff ready for a visit
from the twins.

He's missed them.
So have I.

But when they arrive,
I'm barely there
when we play Clue Jr.
and watch their favorite
Disney movies.

Like a candy wrapper on the ground,
the best part gone.

Again and again
they look in the wrapper,
wanting something to be there.

"Brooklyn, come on,
play with us, play with us!"

Sorry, boys.
Nothing there.
It's just
gone.

Not sure what to do

with myself, I go for a run after school.

I haven't gone far when I look up

at the pale blue sky splattered with clouds.

She taught me to slow down.

To look up and enjoy the view.

To not worry so much about the end result

that I end up missing things along the way.

I stop when a bird flies above me.

I watch him soar, uninhibited and free.

I want to be like that.

I think she does too.

Uninhibited and free,

soaring to new heights,

never standing back, afraid.

In this dream

I'm standing in the toy store,
the aisles filled with
dolls and action figures,
board games and bead kits.

There's a twenty-dollar bill
in my hand so I search the aisles,
looking for something to buy.

How do I choose?
How do I decide?
What would make me happy?

I circle the store,
panic rising in my chest.
I'm supposed to buy something.
I know that.
But it feels like this is a test.
What I choose means something.

After what seems like hours,
I choose a doll
dressed in a pretty pink dress.

An old man with big, red lesions
all over his face and bloodshot eyes
glares at me from behind the register.

"You sure that's what you want?" he asks.

"No.
I don't know.
I don't know what I want."

"It's time to figure it out," he says.

His face starts to change.
The wrinkles fade,
the nose shrinks,
and the old man
morphs into Gabe.

His face is sunken and hollow,
with bulging, bloodshot eyes
and yellow, cracked teeth.

And those sores.
They open, bleed and scab over
until his face is so hideous,
I scream while turning
and running to the door.
But it's locked.

I look behind me.
He's standing there,
holding my notebook.

The notebook that went missing.
The notebook filled with all
my thoughts and feelings
from the past year.
The notebook I want back.

"You want it?" he asks.
"You have to come and get it."

"I can't," I scream.
God, I'm so afraid.

"Don't let fear control you."

Why won't he just stop?
How can I *not* be afraid?

He holds out the notebook
and steps closer.

As I stand there,
looking at him,
wanting desperately
to get away,
I know there's no other solution.

I have to face him.
I have to stop running.

I take a breath.
I take a step.
Another breath.
Another step.

When I'm finally
just inches away,
I reach out and grab the notebook
from his hands.

As I do, he turns from the
gruesome monster
to the Gabe I used to know.
Handsome face.
Thick, brown hair.
Warm green eyes.

"Why?" I ask,
my eyes filled with tears.

"I made you a promise," he says.
"Don't you remember?
We promised to help each other through the pain.
So I had to get you to see, Brooklyn."

"What? That I shouldn't be afraid?"

"Exactly. That you have choices.
Make the right ones.
Don't let fear rule you like it ruled me."

"I'm so sorry, Gabe.
I'm sorry I let you down.
I didn't keep my promise to you."

He reaches out
and puts his finger
to my lips.

"Shhhh. Don't.
No more living in the past.
Okay?"

My insides are trembling.
My outsides, too,
as my brothers call my name,
shaking me to wake up.

He's gone.

I'm back on the couch.
Safe and sound
in my home,
with my notebook
in my hands.

#290

Dear Lucca,

*I've been holding on too long. Afraid to let go.
Afraid to keep living.*

*Afraid.
Afraid.
Afraid.*

*Gabe could see what was happening when I
couldn't. He knew he had to get me to face
my fears.
It must have been hard for him. But I'm thankful
for what he did for me.*

*I hope somewhere, you two are together. That
would make me very happy.*

*Love always,
Brooklyn*

I go in his room

and as I look around,

I think about how we've been trying to keep things the same.

And yet, nothing will ever be the same.

We can stay stuck in the past,

acting like he's going to walk through that door any minute.

Or we can move forward.

Motion vs. stagnation.

Gotta keep things moving.

Ma comes in and asks what I'm doing.

I take a deep breath. And I move forward.

"I thought I might pick up in here," I tell her.

She looks at me. Looks around at the room.

And even though tears fill her eyes, she nods.

"Would it be all right if I help?" she asks.

"Sure. But, Ma, can I ask you something first?

About a girl?"

She smiles. Sits on his bed and pats the spot next to her.

"Absolutely."

When I was little

Mom would read a book to me
every night before bed.
We'd crawl into my twin bed
with the pink and white comforter
and read about Laura on the prairie
or Anne on the Green Gables farm.

I loved her voice as she read the words.
I loved the smell of her strawberries and cream shampoo.
I loved having her all to myself.

When she calls to talk,
I tell her I miss her.
That it's really hard not having her here.
We get a lot of things out
that should have been said a long time ago.
Before she says good-bye,
she says, "I love you, Brooklyn."

It makes me cry and I hang up,
longing for my twin bed
with the pink and white comforter
and the books stacked high on the nightstand.

Those were the days
when dreams were sweet
and life was sweeter still.

So, we're confused.

It's a mixed-up place to be,

on the one hand, falling for each other,

and on the other hand, wanting to stay loyal to Lucca.

Do we have to make a choice?

Is it one or the other?

I remember that kiss,

and how alive I feel when I'm with her.

How could Lucca want anything less than that

for either of us?

It's Sunday.

Comic book day.
For so long,
it was the highlight
of my week.

But he's not here.
And superheroes aren't real.

No matter how hard
I might wish for someone
to jump in and save the day,
it's not going to happen.

It's all up to me now.

I put on the *Joy, Not Sorrow* CD
and jump to the second half.
The half I've never listened to.
I clear off my drawing table.
I find pens and paper.

"Boys, you want to color with me?"

After all, it's not just superheroes
who can choose to use their powers
for the good of mankind.

When I go for a run,

I notice the crocuses peeking out
of the ground.
I take pictures with my phone
and when I get home,
I e-mail them to Brooklyn
with a quick note that says,
"I saw these and thought of you.
Hope you're okay. Can we meet?
Tomorrow morning at the track?"
She's had time.
She's had space.
We need to figure this thing out.
It's lame doing it over e-mail.
What a guy.
But at least I'm doing it.
That's the important thing.

I ride

with the wind at my back,
my legs pumping
hard and fast,
stronger now
than they were a month ago.

I remember
the first day of training
and how I was scared
and excited
all at the same time
to do something
out of my comfort zone.

I said yes.
The nightmares stopped temporarily.
It was a step in the right direction.

Now I understand
I have to keep going.
I have to keep taking
steps in the right direction.
Always going forward.
Never going back.

I breathe
as I walk up the steps
to Gabe's house
and knock.
Scared.
Excited.
Intense.

But that's life.

When Audrey answers the door,
I give her my warmest hello
and remind her who I am.

Then I hug her,
and give her a CD
called *Joy, Not Sorrow*
along with a drawing.
Hyacinths, the flower of hope.

I ask if she has time
to sit and talk.

She does.
And so we do.

At dinner

Pop asks, "How's the training going?"

I look at Ma. She knows. But she keeps quiet.

"It's fine, I guess. A little bumpy."

I look at him. Really look at him.

His hair is thinner. Grayer.

The deep lines in his forehead

tell the story of the past year.

He smiles. "Well, don't give up.

Whatever you do, don't do that."

Ma passes the salad around.

The smell of soup and fresh-made bread.

The comforting hum of conversation.

The sun just setting in the distance.

Man, it feels good.

I glance at Lucca's seat.

Empty for so long.

I think of our hearts.

Empty for so long.

"Don't worry, Pop.

The last thing I'm gonna do is give up."

The twins ask me

to play Chutes and Ladders
before they have to leave tomorrow.

Moving across the squares,
climbing the ladders for good deeds,
sliding down the chutes for bad ones.

When I land on the square
and slide down the longest chute of the game,
Matthew says,
"I hate that one.
Sorry, Brooklyn."

Everyone hates that one.
It's the square nobody wants to land on.
But it's there.
And when you land on it,
you slide down,
practically to the beginning,
and all you can do is keep going,
wishing and hoping
for a ladder to push you back up.

As I think of that,
I realize losing Lucca
was my chute.

After that, I gave up,
so sure a ladder would
never show up.

When it's my turn,
I roll the dice.

I'm not giving up.

To: nicoferrari@remstat.com
From: brooklynbaby@sosmail.com
Subj: Re: Flowers and You

Hi, Nico:

I know we need to talk. Thanks for giving
me some time. I'll see you tomorrow
morning at the track.

And thanks for the pictures. I'm drawing
again. I'll have to draw a crocus next!

Dad's up early

to fly home with the boys.

He's scrambling eggs.
Eggs are his specialty.

"Want some?" he asks.

"No, thanks.
I'm going for a run."

He slides his eggs onto a plate.
Slowly.
Carefully.

He brings them to the table
where I'm sipping orange juice.
They smell good.

"You know," he says, "I get the feeling
something is going on.
I'm not quite sure what,
but I just want you to know I'm here.
If you want to talk."

"Thanks, Daddy.
I actually did want to tell you,
if that offer for a tutor still stands,
I think I could use some help."

He nods.
"Of course. I'll call today."

I watch him take a bite,
his face telling me
he wants to say more.

"Brooklyn," he says.
Slowly.
Carefully.
"If you aren't happy here with me—"

"Dad!"

"I want you to be happy, honey."

I think of him that night,
sobbing because he missed them
in that moment.

Sometimes life is a feast
with eggs Benedict and hollandaise sauce,
waffles and strawberries,
sausage links and hashed brown potatoes.

And sometimes life is scrambled eggs.

In the end,
your stomach gets full all the same.

And years from now,
you may not remember exactly what you ate.

But you'll remember who you ate with.

"Things are fine the way they are," I tell him.
Slowly.
Carefully.
"I just need to work some things out with Nico."

His eyes hug me across the table. "I see."

"Your eggs good?" I ask.

He nods. "Not bad."

And I think,
maybe in the end
that's really
all you can ask for.

I find her on the track,

running as the sun rises in the distance.

I sit in my truck, watching, wanting to join her

but fear keeping a firm hand on my shoulder.

So I just watch.

And wait.

The sun getting brighter.

My desire getting stronger.

Her strides getting slower.

Finally, she stops.

She turns.

She waves.

Fear's hand is still there.

But desire is stronger than fear as it pushes me

right out of my truck.

I zoom in,

frame the shot,
and focus on Nico,
walking toward me.

Photography is all about
perspective.

The light is right.
The angle good.
The subject perfect.

For an instant,
I want to go for it.
I want to take the shot.
I start to move,
my whole body wanting it.

Wanting to capture
what we are
and all we can be
in a single moment.

And yet, as he gets closer,
my perspective changes.

It all changes.

Because no matter how I frame it,
I can't take it all in.
It doesn't fit.

Does it?

Man, she's beautiful.

In the morning light,

her eyes bright and

her cheeks red

as she stands there,

catching her breath.

"Hey," I say.

"Good morning," she says.

"I changed my mind," I say.

"Instead of a run, can I take you to breakfast?"

She shrugs. "Sure."

"Beautiful sunrise, huh?" I say, pointing.

I glance at her and see her face, eyebrows raised.

"Dazzling," she says.

We're back

at the Whistle Stop Café
but how can I eat anything?

There's so much to think about.
To talk about.
To figure out.

We've traveled to hell and back,
different paths but the same journey.

Now we're on a different road.

The people from the photos
smile down upon us
as if to say "safe travels."

But I just don't know
if I'm ready to go.

I take a deep breath

and I tell her
I've been thinking a lot
the past week, about me, about her,
about us, about Lucca.
I tell her
I love how she tries hard to make life fun even when it isn't,
like having a picnic on a stormy day.
I love how she takes time to stop and enjoy the view,
like on our bike rides together.
And I love how she makes me want to do something
other than run all the time.
She makes me want to live, play, have fun.
I tell her
I know it's weird because I'm Lucca's brother
but he would want us to be happy
more than anything else.

And I tell her

I actually know that's true

because he's been visiting me

in my dreams and begging me to help her.

I listen to what he says

trying to take it all in.
He's laying his heart on the table   for me.

It's unbelievable, really,
that after all that's happened,
he wants to do this   with me.

When he says Lucca
has been visiting him in his dreams,
I let out a small gasp.
While Gabe was visiting me,
Lucca was visiting him to   help me.

This means I can
tell him about Gabe
and he'll understand.
He won't think bad things   about me.

I tell her

to please give us a chance,

because we'll always wonder

what would have been if we don't try.

When I'm done telling her all this,

I pause, take a deep breath,

and ask her what she thinks.

I tell him,

I care about him very much.
That he is a real-life Tom Strong,
always trying to help me
and lift me up any way he can.

I tell him

how much I admire his dedication
to do the right thing.
How much I love his kind heart
and passion for the people and things
he cares about.

I tell him

he has so many good qualities.
Just like his brother did.
But different ones.
They're different, he and his brother.
One not better than the other.
Simply different.

When I say this, he turns away from me.
Looks out the window.
Takes a deep breath.

And suddenly I know,
this is what he needed to hear.

We are different.

One isn't better than the other.

Simply different.

"Nico?" she says.

"Look at me."

I turn and face her.

"You don't have to be him. Just be you.

Wonderful, strong, kind you."

And it's what I've needed to hear.

Our food comes

so we're quiet for a while, eating.

When we're done,
I tell him there's one more thing
he needs to know.

I tell him
I've been keeping something from him.
Afraid of what he might think if I told him.
Afraid to share a part of myself with him.
But I'm ready to tell him.

I finally tell him
about Gabe.

When she tells me about Gabe

and how he chased her down

dark hallways and through gray cemeteries,

it all makes sense.

The late-night and early-morning calls,

the fear in her eyes,

the panic in her voice,

Lucca's insistence I help her.

Gabe.

Dream after frightening dream,

she didn't know what to do.

But always, through it all,

I was there, training with her,

a welcome distraction from the horror.

"Has it ended?" I ask.

"I think so," she says.

"We made a promise. A long time ago.

He wanted to see it through.

To help me see how afraid I was to live.

I mean, think about it.

Art has always been my passion.

And I hadn't drawn in a year!"

Tears fill her eyes. Mine too.

I want to reach out to her. Hold her.

But something tells me to wait.

She looks at me. Sadness in her eyes.

"Nico, I have to be honest with you.

I'm making progress. I am.

But this, with you,

I'm just not ready to make a decision yet."

"Progress is good," I tell her.

She smiles. "In a race and in life?"

"Exactly.

And Brooklyn, don't worry.

I'll wait for you at the finish line."

He takes me home,

and I tell him
I'm going to keep training.
But for now,
it needs to be without him,
because I need some time.

"Whatever you need," he says.

When I get out of his truck
I look up.

The clouds are silvery soft.
Looks like rain
will be falling soon.

I turn around and see
he's looking up too.

Then he waves
and drives away.

The extended family is gone

after another successful spaghetti Sunday.

I always miss him on this day.

A little more than other days.

I go to my room and put on an old Killers CD.

And I wait.

When *Smile Like You Mean It*

begins to play,

I feel the cold rush of air,

and the light flickers just enough

so I know he's there.

I let him listen

and right before it ends,

I hold up the book *A Cry for Help*.

"It's your turn, Lucca.

I've done all I can."

The light goes completely out

before the room warms up.

Maybe that's a ghost's way of saying,

"Over and out."

It's Daddy's birthday

I bake him a cake and while it's cooling,
I tell him I have a surprise for him.
But he has to go somewhere with me
to get it.

We go to the animal shelter,
and as we wander through the place,
I know he's wishing he could
take them all home.

"How do I choose, Brooklyn?" he asks.

"I think when it's right, you know," I tell him.
"Like you'll get a feeling it's the right one."

As we wander around,
I spot a Pomeranian.
It takes me back to that day,
when luck was on Lucky's side.
When Nico was on Lucky's side.

It takes my dad a good two hours
to find the right one.

But when we put the
sweet blue heeler named Sadie
in the backseat,
it feels right.

I look at my dad,
a big grin on his face.

He knows he's made
the right decision.
She's the one.

I wish for a little
of that knowing.

Charlie comes over

after school to study for a trig test.

When we're done he says

we should play Guitar Hero.

I tell him I broke the guitar.

He laughs and wants to know

how I managed to do that.

And so I tell him about the day

I heard of Gabe's death.

"What's your theory?" he asks me.

"About what happened to him."

I look out the window.

I think of him and me.

How in some ways,

we really weren't that different.

"I don't know what happened.

But I think he was lost.

He needed an escape.

And my guess is, he didn't intend

to go that far.

It just happened.

Like sometimes I'm running

and I don't want to stop.

I want to keep going,

because deep down inside,

you wonder if there's

a reason to come back, you know?"

Charlie nods. "Dude, can I just say,

it's great to have you back."

I'm standing

on the road,
a car beside me,
wrecked beyond belief.

Their car.

I walk around it,
looking for them,
but it's empty.

The hillside
next to the road
is covered
in forget-me-nots.

Small.
Dainty.
Lovely.

I walk up the hill
and when I reach the top,
I see him.

Lucca.

My legs can't move
fast enough.
When I reach him,
he sweeps me up
and into his arms.

He holds me tightly
for a long,
long time
and I think,
this must be
what heaven's like.

When he lets go,
he gently takes my face
and holds it in his hands,
his loving eyes gripping mine.

"I want you to be happy, Brooklyn.
That's all I've ever wanted."

"But—"

"No. It's that simple.
Don't worry about me.
It's not about me.
It's about you and living your life
in the best possible way."

Just then, I hear footsteps,
and a shadow appears
behind him.

I'd recognize
those footsteps
anywhere.

Gabe.

But this time,
I'm not afraid.

I take Lucca's hand,
and we go to him,
until we stand
face-to-face.

"Every day it's a choice," Gabe says.
"Choose life. Or choose death.
What do you choose?"

I remember the two paths.
The dark, scary one.
The bright, beautiful one.
"Life," I say, my voice shaking.
"I choose life."

And when I speak those words,
Lucca lets go of my hand,
kisses my cheek, and leans down
to whisper in my ear.

"Love is the answer. Not fear."

I stare at him.
How does he know?

I remember the soft feather on my cheek.
The brush of whispers in my hair.
The notes trying to help.
Was he there too?

"We have to go," he says,
interrupting my thoughts.
"I won't forget you, my flower girl."

He blows me a kiss,
and then reaches out
and touches Gabe's shoulder.

In that moment,
light surrounds them.
Radiant and brilliant,
it fills me up with a warmth
like nothing I've ever known.

Lucca leads Gabe down the hill,
where they get into the car,
now without a dent to be seen.

The car drives away slowly
down the long, winding road
laid out before them,
the sun shining brightly
in the distance.

I feel a little piece of my heart
going with them.
Gone forever.

As I wipe a tear
from my cheek,
I hear something.

I look up and suddenly,
the hillside I'm standing on
becomes a shower of butterflies,
in a rainbow of colors.

I spin around
and around
and around,
me and the colors
becoming

one.

It's a beautiful day

so I head out for a bike ride.

I take the road that leads to the beach

and stop at the place we rested that day.

I remember her beautiful eyes.

I remember the dazzling sky.

I remember how she said I was helping her.

The thing I didn't realize at the time

was just how much

she was helping me, too.

I wonder if he knew

that's what would happen.

I bet Lucca knew.

It's a beautiful day

and I feel the need
to get outside and think.

Jackson's Hideway
is an amazing place
with gorgeous, lush greenery all around,
a waterfall,
and a sweet swimming hole,
making it a perfect party place
in the summertime.

Although since Jackson died,
no one dares to jump
from the cliff above anymore.

We changed the name to honor him,
and every time I come here,
I think of him and send a prayer up
for his family and friends.

Today there's no one here,
so I find a rock and open my notebook
filled with letters to Lucca,
reading them,
noticing how the letters
decreased in frequency
over the past couple of months.

When I started,
shortly after he died,
I wrote them every day.
I hurt so bad, I wanted to scream,
but I couldn't,
so my words on the page
became a diary of the pain.

I turn to a blank page,
expecting to write a good-bye letter to him,
surprised at what actually comes out.

Dear Nico,

You opened up your heart to me, and told me how you feel. I know that must have been hard. Scary. For all you knew, I could have gotten up, walked away, and never talked to you again.

Instead, I did the same. I shared everything, including my hesitation. What I've realized is, I'm not hesitant because of YOU. I'm hesitant because of ME. I'm still letting the fear and the pain run my life.

And I don't want to do that anymore.

What I know as sure as the sun will set tonight, painting a canvas of sky blue pink, is that I'm falling in love with you.

I want to give us a chance, Nico. I want to say yes.

I think I'm saying yes.

Love,
Brooklyn

On the ride home

I feel a pull.

The wind whispers to me,

go there,

go there,

go there.

Not sure what I'll find

or why,

I do as the wind tells me.

There's a tap

on my shoulder.

Startled, I jump up,
turning around to find
Jackson's girlfriend, Ava,
standing there.

I breathe a sigh of relief
and smile.
She reaches out and hugs me.

We sit on the rock together,
she and I,
and we talk like long lost friends.

She's going to the local college now,
dating a nice guy she met there.
Her eyes sparkle and shine
with happiness and I feel the longing
in my heart to have that.

It's as if she can read my mind.

"He would want you to be happy," she says.
"You know that, right?"

"I know."

She looks up at the cliff,
where Jackson stood before he jumped.
"I really believe they're at peace
when we're at peace.
They want us to go on,
living the lives we're meant to live."

"You gave me that CD, *Joy, Not Sorrow,*" I say.

"That's what he wants for you, Brooklyn.
He wants you to find joy."

We sit for a while longer,
talking, until the wind picks up,
and it gets cold.

As we walk to the car,
I feel a pull.

The wind whispers to me,
go there,
go there,
go there.

"Why'd you come here today?" I ask.

"The wind whispered to me," she says.
"And I listened."

"I think I know that whisper."

But just to be sure,
I send him a text.

I'm swinging

when she sits down beside me.

"Hi," she says.

"Fancy meeting you here," I say.

She laughs. "Yeah. It is."

I pump my feet hard

while he slows down.
Soon, we're swinging
at the exact same speed.

"How you been?" he asks.

"Good," I say.
"I'm running five miles without walking.
I've even found the zone a couple of times."

"Wow. That's excellent."

"Still, I'm no Tom Strong," she says.

"Yeah, so, what's the deal with Tom Strong?" he asks.

"He's basically my hero," I tell him.

Then I reach over,
handing him the folded letter.

"Should I be worried?"

"No," I say.
"You definitely don't need to worry."

He reads the letter,
and when he's done,
he reaches over and grabs my hand.

"Ready to jump?" he asks.

I look at him,
my heart like
an overfilled balloon,
about to burst.

I smile. "Ready."

And together we jump
a *really*
long way.

I finish the race

and wait for her.

She's worked so hard.

We've come so far.

It was hard at first.

We struggled.

We pounded through the pain.

We struggled some more.

We doubted our abilities.

We questioned our motives.

We found strength in each other.

We told ourselves it would be worth it.

That we'd make it through to the other side.

Happy.

Healed.

Loved.

It was never about the race.

Because as she crosses the finish line,

I know it's not the end.

I grab her,

kiss her wind-chapped face all over,

and spin her around

in the sea of colorful jerseys,

knowing it's only just

the beginning.

Now a glimpse
of Lisa Schroeder's first novel . . .

I Heart You,
You Haunt Me

A Strange Sensation

I can hear my heart
beat
beat
beating
in the darkness
as I try
to go to sleep.

The clock says 12:08.

Mom is asleep by now.

I get up
and go down the stairs
to make hot cocoa.

Will he be there,
waiting for me?

My heart is
beat
beat
beating
faster,
even though
there's no sign of him.

When the hot cocoa is done,
I put marshmallows in.
I stir slowly,
watching them melt
into each other.

I think of Jackson.
His touch,
his kisses,
and the way he looked at me,
with eyes like a green ocean.

I take a sip,
and the cocoa's so hot
it burns my tongue.

Hot.
Cold.
Hot.
Cold.

I shiver.

"Jackson?"

Music Says It All

I sit down
at the kitchen table
and I whisper,
like he is sitting
right across from me.

"Jackson, I know it's you.
I'm not scared.
Maybe I should be, but I'm not.
Whatever you need to do to talk to me,
in your own way, is okay.
I'm not scared.

"Can I see you?
I want to see you."

Nothing happens.

I ask him, "Don't ghosts or spirits or whatever
sometimes show themselves?"

And then
the CD player
on the kitchen counter
starts to play.

3 Doors Down.
Here By Me.

. . . and her second:

Far from You

day five

When I wake up,
early in the morning,
the sun barely
visible
and the blackness
disappearing
just enough
so I can see,
I go outside
and look
for the angel I made.

She's gone,
of course,
covered by
fresh, new snow.

I make another one.

When I'm done,
I don't get up.

I stay there
and dream of
flying away
to the place
where angels
live happily
ever
after.

far from you

My wings lift me
out of the snow,
above the trees,
into the clouds.

My wings carry me
to a place where
all is washed clean
and there is light.

My wings give me
a view of you,
afraid of the shadows,
alone in the cold.

My wings show me
when I'm far from you
it's like an icicle
through my heart.

My wings return me
to the soft patch of snow
where the sun shines brightly
and love brighter still.

a message

And then
the real angel visits again,
her light
illuminating the world
around me.

I try to see her face,
but she appears to be
faceless.

Warmth engulfs
and soothes me,
like a warm bubble bath
on a cold winter's night.

She whispers my name.

"Alice."

I can't make my lips
say her name.

"Don't give up," she says so softly,
I can hardly hear her.
"Help is coming."

Then, as quickly
as she appeared,
she's gone again.

ABOUT THE AUTHOR

LISA SCHRODER is the author of *Far from You* and *I Heart You, You Haunt Me*, a 2009 ALA Quick Pick for Reluctant Young Adult Readers. She loves to write in verse because it allows her to really get at the emotional core of the story. She is grateful to all of the people who have read her books and told their friends about them, since being an author is more fun than ponies or water slides (most of the time, anyway). Lisa lives in Oregon with her husband and two sons. You can visit her online at LisaSchroederBooks.com.